ONLY ONE WAY OUT

As she began to straighten up he moved, as fast as or faster than he ever had before in his life.

With one swoop he had the hay rake in hand, and with a forward lunge he thrust it out behind her back. He pulled with all his might from a position on his knees. She was flying straight toward him.

He gripped her as tightly as he could while he slipped his left hand down in between them, searching for her apron pocket.

In another second he would have the keys. . . .

DON'T MISS THESE
ALL-ACTION WESTERN SERIES
FROM THE BERKLEY PUBLISHING GROUP

THE GUNSMITH by J. R. Roberts
Clint Adams was a legend among lawmen, outlaws, and ladies. They called him . . . the Gunsmith.

LONGARM by Tabor Evans
The popular long-running series about U.S. Deputy Marshal Long—his life, his loves, his fight for justice.

LONE STAR by Wesley Ellis
The blazing adventures of Jessica Starbuck and the martial arts master, Ki. Over eight million copies in print.

SLOCUM by Jake Logan
Today's longest-running action Western. John Slocum rides a deadly trail of hot blood and cold steel.

◄► TABOR EVANS ◄►

LONGARM

AND THE GALLAGHER GANG

J

JOVE BOOKS, NEW YORK

LONGARM AND THE GALLAGHER GANG

A Jove Book / published by arrangement with
the author

PRINTING HISTORY
Jove edition / August 1994

ISBN: 0-515-11435-9

A JOVE BOOK®
Jove Books are published by The Berkley Publishing Group,
200 Madison Avenue, New York, New York 10016.
JOVE and the "J" design are trademarks belonging to Jove Publications, Inc.

PRINTED IN THE UNITED STATES OF AMERICA

10 9 8 7 6 5 4 3 2 1

LONGARM

AND THE GALLAGHER GANG

Chapter 1

As Longarm sat in the sheriff's office in Wichita Falls, Texas, he decided he was nearly as tired as he'd ever been sober and out of bed. For two weeks he'd hunted an elusive horse thief named Genuine Bob Guest through the badlands of the Oklahoma Territory, finally bottling him up in a box canyon where they had attempted to see who could go the longest without food or water. Longarm couldn't pry Genuine Bob out of his concealed position, and Genuine Bob couldn't get by Longarm, so it had settled down to a war of attrition with the August sun and the lack of water and food the main weapons. In the end Longarm had won, mainly because he could go without sleep longer than Genuine Bob. He'd taken the horse thief early one morning, slipping up on him and manacling his hands together before he was completely awake.

Once caught, Genuine Bob had been an amiable prisoner, mainly because he, like most of the lawbreakers in the territories Longarm operated in, knew that Deputy

U.S. Marshal Custis Long was truly the long arm of the law, and that once you were caught you might as well go along quietly. Your other choice was to go along laid across the back of your horse with your lifeless arms and legs hanging down on either side of your mount.

Genuine Bob had had three stolen horses with him when Longarm ran him to ground, and he had been more than glad to help herd them into Wichita Falls and tell Longarm where they rightfully belonged. In return Longarm had taken Genuine Bob into a saloon before he turned him into the sheriff's office, letting him get a pretty good load on at government expense before he faced the closeness of a jail cell.

After that Longarm expected to take the first train out that would point him toward his home in Denver, sleeping the whole way. But the sheriff in Wichita Falls, Kyle Greenwood, had a message for him. Greenwood had known Longarm for most of the years he'd been a deputy federal marshal. "They's a lady 'bout ten miles out of town on the Lawton road," he said, "come in here and give me a message for you 'bout the Gallagher gang."

Longarm was instantly alert. "The Gallagher gang?" he said. "How the hell would some country lady know anything about them desperadoes?" The Gallagher gang was a bunch that had anywhere from eight to a dozen members. They'd robbed gold shipments and banks in New Mexico, Arizona, and Colorado, and stolen livestock in half a dozen states and territories. Longarm had managed to put three of the gang in prison or underground, but the three brothers, Rufus, Clem, and Vern, had so far eluded him. He'd been after the gang for almost two years, and it was a blow to his pride that he hadn't made more progress against them. If there was one bunch he thoroughly despised, it was the Gallaghers. While Genuine Bob was a horse thief and a shady character, the Gallaghers were murderers and rapists and, as far as Longarm was concerned, mean to the bone. They were the scum of the outlaw world, among the worst of the thieves and murderers and bandits that he'd hunted. For him they were a personal crusade. The news from Kyle Greenwood came as a surprise because the Gallaghers hadn't been heard from in better than six months. In fact Longarm had halfway begun to hope that they'd finally fled to Mexico. What had made them so difficult to catch was the fear they inspired, so that it was hard to get accurate information about their activities and what they looked like. Not to mention the fact that they hit with quick, well-planned raids and then disappeared.

Usually leaving no witnesses. Their trademark was fire. If they robbed a ranch of cattle or horses, they would burn the ranch house and the barns. If they robbed a bank, they would try to set it afire along with half the town it was in. They would even burn the wagons of the stores they looted, or the armed vehicles carrying the bullion they stole from the gold mines.

Dynamite was another trademark. What they couldn't burn they blew up.

Sheriff Greenwood went on. "I don't know how she knows about the Gallaghers. She just showed up here about a week ago. Said she was in town laying in supplies and heard you was hereabouts and wanted to give you some information."

"How in hell would she know my whereabouts?"

Greenwood smiled slightly. "Hell, Custis, you been around here near two weeks running down Bob Guest. You're kind of like a sandstorm, a little hard not to notice."

3

"What's this lady's name?"

"Lily Gail Wharton."

"How come she came in and not her husband?"

"She's a widder lady is how come. Moved here about a year ago and took up a place somebody else had let go to the bank. Runs a few cattle."

"A widow lady making it on her own on a ranch?"

"She's got some part-time hired help. But it's a good little property. Hell, raising cattle ain't all as hard as ranchers make it out to be. Turn 'em out on good grass most of the year. Worm 'em and cut 'em in the spring, market 'em in the fall, or feed them through the winter. She don't have to pay wages more than a month out of the year."

"I just can't see how some old widow woman knows aught about the Gallaghers."

Greenwood got a little gleam in his eyes. "She ain't exactly some *old* widow woman, Custis. She's a widow, but she's a mighty young one and a mighty toothsome one at that. She's had every young buck in three counties slobbering around her kitchen door, I hear, but she ain't give none of them so much as a peek inside. Naturally, knowing yore reputation with the ladies, I figured you'd be interested for more reason than the Gallaghers."

Longarm gave him a thoughtful look. "Kyle, was I you I wouldn't be making no comments about trafficking in womenfolk."

Greenwood smiled. "I'm an old married man. Don't know what you're talking about."

"*Now* you're married. Why don't you invite me home for supper sometime, Kyle. And then let's me and you talk about some of them adventures we got up to in front of your wife. Want to do that, Kyle?"

4

Greenwood got a slightly alarmed look on his face. "Don't even joke like that, Custis. That's not funny."

Longarm stood up from where he'd been sitting on the side of Greenwood's desk. He was a tall man, even without his high-heeled boots, a little over six feet. He was spare and lean except in his shoulders, upper arms, and hands. He sat a horse like a feather, with 190 pounds of gristle and bone and suntanned hide and muscle. His face was slashed with a wide mouth and his brown eyes were big, but mostly drawn down from having squinted into too many suns. His weathered face said he might have been forty years of age, but he moved and acted ten years younger than that. He was deceptively friendly-looking. Even some men who'd been killed five seconds later had thought he was smiling at them benignly. His weaknesses were women and poker and horse-trading, in no particular order of importance.

Longarm smiled. "So you reckon I ought to go out there and sort of comfort this widow woman. Seeing as how you are now out to pasture."

Greenwood leaned back in his chair and entwined his hands behind his head. "Well, there is that. But she also claimed to have some knowledge about the Gallaghers."

"Why didn't she tell you what it was?"

Greenwood gave him a sour look. "I would reckon the woman knows my authority stops at the county line. Hell, I don't think she's even in this county. But she specifically said she'd heard there was a deputy U.S. marshal in these parts."

"She didn't call me by name?"

Greenwood thought a moment, then shook his head. "I don't remember it. I think *I* said Deputy Marshal Long. Or maybe *she* said it. No, because she didn't say Deputy.

Probably didn't know you wasn't no exalted big chief marshal like yore boss, Billy Vail."

"Hell, I'm dead on my feet. I was thinking of taking the train and sleeping all the way home."

"Hell, you're damn near halfway to Lawton when you get to her place. And the train out of Lawton goes up to Oklahoma City. You got a straight shot from there to Denver." He gave Longarm a wink. "Besides, the Widder Lily Gail Wharton might just offer you a bed for the night."

Longarm yawned. "I guess I might as well. That's an army horse I'm riding out there. There's a post in Lawton where I can return him." As a deputy U.S. marshal Longarm could requisition arms, ammunition, supplies, or mounts from any government installation anywhere.

Greenwood said, "Course I don't see her having anything will help you much. Hell, even the army couldn't catch them damn Gallaghers."

Longarm didn't say anything. He was thinking about the time, a little less than a year ago, when the Gallaghers had attacked a small U.S. Cavalry outpost and made off with a supply of arms and ammunition. Some said they'd gotten away with a couple of pieces of field artillery, but that rumor had turned out to be false. Longarm had been in on the later stages of the hunt, when they'd thought they had the gang boxed up in the Ouchita Mountains of eastern Oklahoma Territory. To this day he still wondered how the Gallaghers had gotten away. One moment the cavalry had been ready to spring the trap shut, and the next moment the fox had vanished. The hundred men of the catch party had searched every crevice, every nook, every cave, every possible hiding place they could find. But it had been in vain. The

Gallaghers and their bunch had slipped through their fingers. Longarm had privately concluded that there'd been a few links in the encircling chain, that some money had changed hands and an open gate had been created. Army privates, after all, only made twenty-one dollars a month, and a few hundred dollars in bribe money would open a lot of doors.

Now he said, "Well, I guess I'll ride that way, Kyle. Take good care of ol' Genuine Bob. He ain't a real bad hombre."

"How come him to call himself Genuine Bob?"

Longarm shrugged. "I guess it goes back to when he was kind of a nearly genuine horse trader. He said there were so many Honest Bobs and Honest Johns and Honest Jims that he was just looking for a way to kind of call attention to himself."

Kyle Greenwood laughed slightly. "Well, I guess he done that when he went to trading other folks' horses."

"And the name stuck. I got to be making tracks, Kyle."

"Think of me when you are, uh, asking Lily Gail Wharton some *hard* questions."

"You got a foul mind, Kyle. A foul mind."

It was still early afternoon. After an hour and a half of riding Longarm began looking for the widow's ranch. Kyle had described her house as white, freshly painted, with a red barn just behind. Kyle had said, "Figure how many fresh-painted white ranch houses you've seen around here in the last blue moon and you can figure how hard it's gonna be to spot."

The ranch house was only supposed to be a half mile off the main road. He finally spotted it on a little knoll that rose out of the rolling, grassy prairie. He turned the

7

rough-gaited cavalry horse in between a couple of posts that marked a wagon track leading up to the house and kicked the animal into a trot. It was a mistake he'd made several times before, and he quickly nudged the horse's flanks and put him into a lope. Riding the horse, he reckoned, was as close to rocking in a broken-legged chair as he'd ever come. If he had two such horses, he'd kill one for meat and sell the other to his worst enemy.

He rode up in front of the small frame house and stopped for a moment to survey it. Except for the paint it was an ordinary ranch house for the time and the place—except that it was the house of a woman running a ranch. He looked around the fields. There didn't appear to be a garden out back of the house or any cornfields. Neither did he see many cattle. If the woman was going to make a living out of the place, somebody was going to have to teach her a little more about ranching. To ranch you needed cattle, and to feed cattle through eastern Oklahoma's harsh winters you needed either hay fields or oats or corn. This ranch didn't appear to have any of what was needed. The lack of a kitchen garden especially surprised him. He'd never known a farm or ranch wife who hadn't insisted on one. He had an idea this was a widow who was very near to giving up the ranching business and heading back for civilization to find herself another husband. He wondered if she had any children. If she did, they'd be young judging by the way Kyle Greenwood had described her.

His arrival didn't appear to have been noticed, and he saw no workers about the place. He stood up in his stirrups and called, "Hello, the house!"

Nothing happened, and he was about to do it again when the front door, guarded by a small wooden porch, was suddenly pulled back and a young woman stepped out into the light. She shaded her eyes with her hand and looked his way. She said, "Yes? Who is it?"

She was ten yards away and partly in the shadow of the porch, but Longarm had spotted less comely women than her at twice the distance and in full dark of night. He let his horse walk forward. Taking off his hat, he said, "Would you be Missus Lily Gail Wharton?"

"Who would be asking?"

He was only a few yards from the porch and could see her clearly. She was wearing a yellow print gingham frock that went very well with her green eyes and her light brown, bouncy curls. She had a heart-shaped face with full ruby lips and rouged cheeks. She didn't look any more like a ranch wife than her place looked like a working ranch. But Longarm's eyes were on the flare of her hips and the swell of her breasts, which seemed to want to come flowing over the top of a square-cut neckline that was so low he could see her cleavage. He said, "Ma'am, my name is Custis Long. I'm a deputy United States marshal. The sheriff in Wichita Falls, Kyle Greenwood, said—"

She clapped her hands together, her face lit up, and she seemed to almost jump in the air in a little hop. "Oh, goody!" she said. "I was so a-hopin' you'd git my message an' come. Oh, this is just so wonderful! Marshal, you just step down and come right on in here in this house and let me make you a welcome."

As he dismounted, he thought it was a great shame that such long periods of time had to pass between greetings like that from such beautiful, voluptuous women. Come to think of it, he'd never quite had a greeting like that. Which was another hardship that life had visited on him for no good reason he could think of.

He walked the couple of steps and mounted the porch. He smiled as big as he thought a deputy marshal ought to. "Well, howdy, ma'am. I don't know what it is you've got to tell me, but I already feel like this trip ain't been wasted."

He followed her into the coolness of her house, admiring her from behind and wishing her dress wasn't so long so he might catch a glimpse of an ankle or even a slim calf.

She led him into the parlor and sat him down. "I'm just going to make us a big pitcher of lemonade," she said. "I've got some cool well water, and it ought to be mighty refreshing after your long ride in this hot sun."

"Yes," he said, wondering why women always insisted on giving a man lemonade. "That would go down mighty good." Of course anybody that knew anything about the heat knew the idea was to raise the body temperature with a few shots of whiskey so the air wouldn't seem so hot to the skin. But damn few women he ever met had ever learned that.

But when she returned from the kitchen she was bearing a tray with a pitcher of lemonade, two glasses, and a bottle of whiskey on it. She set it on a little low, ornate table that was in front of the divan where she'd seated him. "There! I reckon you wouldn't take it amiss to have a little long sweetenin' in with your lemonade. I know that'd be the only way my husband would have taken it, God rest his soul. He'd of knocked me flyin' if I'd fetched him in *straight* lemonade. Woulda said, 'Who's that fer—the kids? We ain't got none.' " She laughed girlishly. "Now you can help yourself."

She sat down in a little parlor chair right across from him. As she leaned forward to pour the lemonade, he could not help admiring the view down her neckline. Somehow he had the feeling she was doing it on purpose; after all, she was a widow who'd been without for who knows how long. He said, picking up the bottle of whiskey and adding a healthy pour to his glass of lemonade, "Ma'am, you are as good-a-hearted person as I've met in I don't know when. I reckon this is gonna go down mighty fine."

She was fanning herself with a little cardboard fan with a wooden handle on it and a picture of a a snow-topped mountain on one side. "It *is* hot, ain't it?" Her frock buttoned down the front, and he could see where the top button at her square-cut neckline had somehow worked itself about halfway undone.

He took a long drink of the lemonade and the whiskey, and then set his half-empty glass back down on the tray. "Aw, me. That hits the spot."

She poured a little more lemonade in his glass, and then, even without him asking, added an equal amount of whiskey to it. Now here, he thought, was something, a respectable widow woman actually condoning the drinking of whiskey, and not only condoning, but aiding. Clearly she knew how to treat a man.

But then, with a wrench, he jerked himself back to his job. He'd come to ask this woman what she knew about the Gallaghers, not to drink whiskey and admire her breasts. He said, "Missus Wharton, you—"

"Please call me Lily Gail. Ever'body does."

It wasn't professional of him, but he said, "Well, Lily Gail, you mentioned to Kyle Greenwood that you might have some information for me about a bunch of outlaws called the Gallaghers. Is that right?"

She was about to take a delicate sip of lemonade sweetened with a discreet amount of whiskey. At his question she lowered her glass and looked uncertain. She said hesitantly, "Well . . . I think I can. I'm not right sure. See, it more involved my husband—I mean my late husband—than it did me."

Longarm could see the thought of her husband had somewhat unnerved her. He said gently, "How long have you been without your husband, Lily Gail?"

She blinked for a second as she composed herself. "Let's see. This is August. Since February. Six months?" She looked up at him.

"Uh, might I ask what, what was, uh, the, the cause of his, his, uh . . ."

She said matter-of-factly, "A horse kicked him. We hadn't no more than taken this place up, not even a year from the time we moved the first stick of furniture into this parlor or put a steer in a pasture, than he was taken from us, raised up to Paradise."

"We? Do ya'll have little ones?"

She smoothed her lap with her hands. "Well, no. And more the shame of it. You might have called Bob and me newlyweds. By we, I mean him and me and, I guess, the ones we expected to come along in time."

"Yes," he said gently. He took another sip of his whiskey and lemonade, wondering how he could get back on the subject that had brought him out in the first place without bringing up painful matters. He said, "Missus— excuse me, I can't seem to get that right." He leaned forward and put an emphasis on her name. "Excuse me, *Lily Gail*, what was it you were going to tell me about the Gallaghers?"

She put her hand to her breast and looked away for a second. When she turned back to him she said, "Well, all I can tell you is what I know, which, I must hasten to add, mayn't be that much, you understand, because it was mainly with my husband."

He nodded, getting a little impatient. "Yes, ma'am."

She fanned herself again, and this time the top button did come undone, revealing a little more than an inch of lace-trimmed camisole. She didn't seem to notice. She said, "Well, one day these men came. 'Bout a year ago? Not too long after we were here. Was a bunch of them, maybe a half a dozen. An' my husband went out to meet them, out there in the yard. Naturally I was peekin' out the winder and watchin' and, oh, my, Marshal, they was a rough-lookin' bunch. Had a wagon with them that was pulled by four mules. Never will forget that. Wagon was loaded way up high and covered with a tarpaulin. You could tell it was heavy by the way it cut ruts in the ground. Is the lemonade all right?"

"Just fine, Lily Gail. You go right ahead."

She fanned herself again. "Well, first thing I knew the whole bunch of them, my husband included, went riding off toward a back pasture that's over that little rise of ground back yonder. They's a little valley down there with some caves and a crick. Of course I never thought to follow them. That wouldn't have done. But I watched out the kitchen door, and they was gone better than an hour. Maybe two. An' funny thing about it, wasn't all of them come back. And that wagon was empty. Now what do you suppose about that?"

Longarm said, "Well, I'd guess that they unloaded the wagon back in those caves or somewhere. Did you ever go look?"

She put her hand to her mouth. "Oh, my, no! My husband come in looking just pleased as punch. An' you know what? He had a hunnert dollars in his hand! A whole hunnert dollars! Can you imagine that?"

"Well, yes," Longman said dryly, "I guess I can. And you think it was the Gallaghers that came and hid some stuff on your property?"

A little frown creased her face. "Well, it wasn't only just that. The funny thing was that all of a sudden we had two hired hands. And I could have sworn they was some of the ones that first rode up in our yard. Rough-looking men, you know."

"You think they stayed behind when the others left with the wagon?" His interest was starting to grow.

"I didn't know what to think." She smoothed her sleek hair with a plumpish hand. "Course I didn't ask my husband about them. He made it clear he wouldn't have that. They slept in the barn and I cooked for them and he taken their meals out to them. I never did see them doin' much work to speak of. But then one day they was a detachment of soldiers come by. Them kind on horses."

"Cavalry."

"Yes. The ones with the gold stripes down their legs. They come by and spoke with my husband out in the front yard, and that was one of the first times I ever seen them men hitting a lick of work. They commenced fixing the corral fence like it would burn up if they didn't stay right after it. Funny thing about that was they wasn't nothing wrong with the fence."

"I see," Longarm said slowly. He was starting to get an idea of how the Gallaghers could disappear so easily. "Then what happened?"

She shrugged. "Well, nothing. After a time, when they was no more soldiers coming by, the two hired hands just up and left. Not long after that my husband got kilt." She looked sad for a moment, but then her face suddenly brightened. "But it wasn't that he didn't do right by me. Deputy, you won't believe this, but I found near four hundred dollars hid in his side of the mattress. You know how you'll air out a mattress after a body has died on it? Well, when I done that, that money commenced to fall out of that mattress like it was snowing."

Longarm said, "I'm not all that surprised." He poured himself a little more whiskey. So that was how the Widow Lily Gail Wharton had managed to hang on so long. You could ranch for quite a time on four hundred dollars. "Lily Gail, what do you know about the Gallaghers?"

She looked at him solemnly. "Just what I've heard. That they are well-poisoners and barn-burners and will rob anybody."

"Well, all this took place nearly a year ago." His mind turned back thinking that that was just about the time the Gallaghers had slipped the army's trap and disappeared. And the Ouchita Mountains weren't all that far from where he was sitting.

She nodded. "Yes, I guess it was."

"Why have you waited so long to come forward?"

She fluttered her hands around her hair. "Well, lordy, I'm just a woman. What would I know? I mean, while my husband was alive. And then he got kicked by that horse and that was the last of him. Then they was the funeral and all. I swear, they was so much to think about—trying to think what I should do and how to go about it—that the whole shootin' match just clean went out of my head. An' then I heered they was a federal marshal come to town an' I thought, well, maybe I ought to tell you 'bout it. I don't know what it's worth. But I thought I'd make the effort. I ast around about you when I was in town Saturday, but they said you was gone, so I stopped in at the sheriff's." She let her hands go up and down in the air. "And here you are."

"Yeah," he said, "here I am." For a second he sat staring at her, trying to decide if she'd really told him anything that would help. Knowing how the Gallaghers had evaded the army trap the year before wasn't a lot of help now. It would come in handy if the circumstance ever came up again, but he doubted it would. They had just sort of disappeared, dropping off by ones and twos to pose as ranch and farm workers. Which wouldn't have been all that difficult. Where they didn't have family or friends they had money to grease their way. Likely Longarm and the cavalry and the other law officers had been chasing one man leading a string of horses in the mountains. He would have turned the horses loose and hidden himself in a cave or something. Maybe even run off somehow. It didn't much matter. Not anymore. Now Longarm said, "Lily Gail, you've never gone to see what they hid back in your little caves and crevices?"

"Well, no," she said slowly. She was idly playing with the second button on the bosom of her dress. Seeming almost unconscious of what she was doing, she unbuttoned it, and then the next one. The neck of her camisole was cut very low, and the gingham fell away to reveal the skin of her milky white breasts. Longarm could feel his breath coming a little faster. She picked up the fan and began to stir the air around her, saying, "My, it is hot, ain't it?"

"I reckon," Longarm managed to say. His throat was getting so tight he could barely get the words out. "How come you didn't get curious and have a look? I mean, after your husband got killed."

"Well, after Bob got kilt I taken him back home to Arkansas for the funeral. I knowed he'd want to be buried with his kin. That took a while, what with the visiting and all. And then it is a ways back to those caves and I don't ride a horse. And a buggy . . ." She shrugged. "I just wasn't all that curious, Marshal." She looked up at him with her big, green eyes. "Was that wrong of me?"

"No, no, no," he said. But he was having a hard time concentrating on the words he was saying. Her hand had strayed back to her bosom and was playing with the fourth button. "No, I see why it wouldn't have any interest for you, what with your own, uh, troubles to, uh, deal with."

She leaned over and picked up the bottle of whiskey. "I do declare, Marshal, yore glass is dry."

Now the linen of her white camisole fell away from her breasts, and he could see the pink rosettes and the beginning of the nipples that crowned them. His mouth had gone dry. He had been out hunting Genuine Bob for a long time and this was all happening so fast. She glanced up at him as she was pouring the whiskey. "You need to say when," she said.

"Now," he said hoarsely. "Right now. Just as quick as we can." Almost unconsciously, he put his hand out and touched her forearm.

She pulled back, still holding the bottle of whiskey. Her eyes were wide and innocent. "Why, Marshal Long, whatever do you mean?"

He stared at her, perplexed. If he'd gotten his signals wrong, it was a long time since he'd made such a mistake. The pulse at his temple was going like a triphammer. He said, "What do you think I mean? You are sitting there half undressed. What do you reckon I got in my mind?"

She said, "Well, I never!" She opened her mouth and ran her plump little tongue over her full, pouty lips. "It's just hot. I don't see how something like that can be misunderstood about a body. My goodness!"

He sat back and took a deep breath and then let it out slowly. "Forgive me, Missus Wharton. I apologize."

"You ain't gonna call me Lily Gail no more?"

He stared at her, totally confused. "What is going on here, Lily Gail? I mean, I'm wearing a badge, but I'm also a man. I'm sorry if I misunderstood, but I reckon I better get out of here. I'm obliged for the information."

She said, "Oh, no! Not just yet. It's so seldom I get a handsome gentleman caller. And you ain't finished your drink." She took up the pitcher of lemonade and filled up the glass that was already half whiskey. She handed him the glass, leaning forward as she did so that her breasts almost fell free of the restraints of her camisole. "You don't need to rush off. I been kind of hoping you'd stay for supper. I got a big beef roast in the cold cellar I need to get cooked."

He took the glass, but said, "Really, Lily Gail, I don't reckon I better."

"Oh, pshaw. You ain't got no better place to go on a hot afternoon like this. You just set there and drink yore drink an' I'll nip out to the kitchen and get that joint of beef on to cook."

He was about to make another excuse for leaving when she casually unbuttoned one more button. It was almost down to her waist now, and her full breasts, covered by just the thin linen of her camisole top, were exposed. He could see her nipples straining against the light material, big and hard, looking like ripe strawberries. He didn't know what was going on, but he knew he wasn't quite ready to leave. He said a little unsteadily, "Yes, you go ahead and do that. I'll just sit here."

She got up, her dress now so loose that it was almost falling off one shoulder, and disappeared through a door on the far side of the room. He reckoned it to be the kitchen, but he was so agitated he scarcely paid any attention at all. He thought to himself that he had never been quite so confused about a woman in all his life. He'd had women come at him making no bones about it, and he'd had women that needed a bit of wooing, but he'd never had one who on the face of the matter seemed to be inviting him in, and then so suddenly seemed to be slamming the door in his face. He knew he hadn't had enough whiskey to be anywhere near drunk, but he sure as hell felt as confused as he ever had about one subject, especially since that subject was one he'd always considered himself a fair hand at. He didn't know if this particular female was all that innocent, or if she was just having sport with him.

"Hell!" he said aloud, and sipped at his drink. Then he said aloud again, "Custis, if you had any sense, which you ain't when you get the smell of poontang in your nostrils, you would get the hell up and get on your horse and ride on down the road."

But he knew he wouldn't. Not as long as there was a chance that this delectable bit of goods wasn't leading him down the primrose path. Or even if she was, that there'd be something worth having when they got to the end of the path. Maybe it was just that she was a widow woman and he felt it was unseemly for her to appear too eager. Maybe she just needed some urging. But he was an officer of the law, a federal officer, and there was a limit to just how far he could go in his urging.

Then he heard a voice, calling him. He sat still, stock-still. The voice was low and soft and was coming from the room she'd disappeared into. She was saying, "Marshal, oh, Marshal . . . Would you come here for just a minute. I got somethin' I want to show you. . . ."

He took a quick gulp of his drink and stood up a little unsteadily. He could feel his heart beating rapidly. There was a sound in that voice that didn't make him think she was calling to ask him to go outside and fetch in some kindling wood.

"Oh, Marshal . . . I got something to show you. . . ." The voice went up and down like a cat purring.

He went around the little table and crossed the room in four or five strides.

The door that he had thought led to the kitchen, the one she'd disappeared through, didn't turn out to lead to a kitchen after all. It was a room with a bed in it. She was lying on the bed naked. Her hair was spread on the pillow her head was resting on, and she had her arms outflung and her legs apart. He stood in the door frame, staring at her. Her skin was very white, making the pink of her nipples stand out ever more. The light brown of her thatch curled and rose with the mound that made a little hump just above where her legs joined. Then the curly little hairs ran down between her legs. He knew that they would be silken and soft, and he knew that she would already be warm and wet.

He said, barely able to speak his chest was so tight, "I see it wasn't a joint of beef you were putting on to cook."

She put her hands down to herself, parting the thatch of curly hair, and then pulling back the lips so that he could see the pink inside. She said, "Is it done?"

He was taking off his gunbelt as fast as he could, letting it fall to the floor. Then he was ripping off his shirt and, standing on first one foot and then the other, jerking his boots off. His jeans followed and he went to her, walking to her side of the bed.

Chapter 2

She half rose and turned toward him as he came to the side of the bed. She reached out with both hands and took his excited member in her fingers, stroking it. Then, with a little forward thrust of her head, she took him inside her mouth, taking him so deep he wondered where it was going. He could see her lips pouting out so far they were inside his own hair. Rhythmically, she worked her head back and forth, sliding him in and out with such warmth and smoothness that he could feel the tingle beginning at his toes and running all up and down his body. He shuddered and gritted out, "You better stop. Oh, hell, you better quit. I'm gonna—"

He pulled himself free of her and crawled up on the bed as she lay back. She guided him inside her and he felt himself going deep, deep, deep. For a second he lay still and panted. Then he put his big hands under her buttocks and began to lift. She flung her arms around his neck as he rose up to his knees, still holding her clamped to him. Then, one foot at a time, he got to his feet. Her arms were around his neck and her legs were clamped and locked around his waist. He stepped down from the bed and began to walk around the room with her. She had her head thrown back, her mouth open, sighing and breathing hard. Using her grip around his neck, she held herself while she used her legs to pull herself back and forth against the piston of his member. She made a long sigh, and then a sort of suppressed scream, and began to arch her back. It lasted and lasted and lasted. Finally, she made a deep keening noise and went limp.

But only for a second. As he was backing toward the bed she was once again thrusting herself at him, pushing him toward his own limit. He felt the edge of the bed at the back of his knees, and he fell backwards. She rode him all the way down, pausing only to sweep her legs wide so they wouldn't be caught under his back.

And then she was over him, rotating, twisting, thrusting. Her small breasts with their June-strawberry nipples were right over his face. One of them was suddenly in his mouth. He was trying to hold on to the exquisite feeling for as long as he could. He could feel her sweet, hot breath on his face, and then her tongue was in his eye and he could hold it no longer. He exploded.

It seemed to go on and on and she was going with him. He could dimly hear her screaming, feel with his hands her back arching, feel her nails on his chest.

And then it was no more. He went limp and she slumped down on him, much heavier now than she had been when he'd picked her up and carried her around the room. He was gasping. He felt drained. He couldn't have picked up a whiskey glass if he'd been dying of thirst. His voice croaked. He said, "Oh, my goodness, Lily Gail, you are really something. You cooked a piece of meat, all right, but it wasn't no joint of beef."

She half raised up and began kissing him on the chest, working her way slowly up to his mouth. "Am I under arrest, Marshal?"

"Yeah," he said. "You stole a load off me I don't think a team of mules could haul off."

He could feel her fingers exploring his limp member and his testicle sac. He said, "Not yet, honey. Ah, mercy, not yet. It's my other gun that's made out of steel. This one is just a single-shot."

She pouted. "But I want some more."

"In a minute. You got to let me rest."

"Then do this." She took his hand and guided his index finger down to where she was warm and wet, to a little secret pip that rose at the end of the pink cave. He began to slowly caress it, feeling it come rising up out of its hood. Within a moment her breathing was starting to come fast, her fingers began digging into his chest, and her mouth and tongue sought his.

He marveled, feeling himself aroused, as her passion rose higher and higher. She was thrusting her hips rhythmically against his finger, her arms clamped around his neck, her mouth glued to his. And then she took her lips away to sigh and then scream, and her back arched and then she was biting and kissing him, her hands pulling his body into hers. Finally she subsided and lay limp again.

He said softly, "Lily Gail, you are some kind of girl. I thought *I* liked it. But you . . ."

She raised up and put her face over his, her green eyes looking innocent and babyish. "Ain't we supposed to?"

"Oh, yes," he said. "Oh, yes. Just ain't enough women realize it to suit me."

23

"Then they don't know what they missing."

For a while they lay quietly and then she stirred beside him and began kissing him on the stomach. He felt her lips teasing the skin of his member. He said, "Lily Gail, I can't go just yet. Damn, I never thought I'd hear myself saying that, but girl, I'm fifteen or twenty years older than you."

She suddenly got up and got out of bed. She said, "I'll bring you some whiskey. That'll put the lead back in your pencil."

He watched her as she walked across the floor to the door. Lord, he thought, she did have a figure to make a man's mouth water, with just enough of a sheen of baby fat to make her sleek and soft. She had a beautifully rounded little bottom and her small breasts tilted up at just the right angle. Her legs were sleek and straight and her waist tucked in just as perfectly as you could draw it on paper.

And that thing between her legs. He could still feel the sensation. It seemed to have tiny little fingers inside it that massaged and milked you until it got every drop out of a man. He shook his head and said, "Whew!" He knew for damn certain where he was spending this night. And if she was willing, he might have to delay his trip back to Colorado for a few days. He did not believe he had ever run across a woman quite like her. She was as expert as they came, but she still looked so innocent you'd swear she was a virgin. He looked down his flat belly and cursed his organ for not being ready for duty when called upon. "You sonofabitch, don't ever come crying to me you let this chance get away. Just think of the dry spell we been through and maybe that will get your head up."

She came back with a water glass full of amber liquid. He sat up and swung his legs over the side of the bed.

"Hell, Lily Gail, I can't drink that much whiskey, not and walk, much less do anything else."

She said, "Lots of it is lemonade."

"What'd you do that for?"

"Oh, I just never thought. Drink it down now, so we can play some more."

He sipped at the drink, wondering why anyone wanted to waste the taste of good whisky with lemon squeezings. It tasted a little tart, but he put that down to the lemons. She was standing right in front of him, and he put out his hand and stroked the mound that was forested with the silky hair. He said, "I believe that may be the most beautiful thing on the face of the earth."

She came closer, reaching down to pull the lips apart. He could smell the musk of her as strong as a feeling. She said, "Hurry up with that drink. I'm gettin' all excited. Drain it down."

He turned the glass up and whisked it down his throat. The whiskey scarcely seemed to have any bite at all. As he lowered the glass she pressed the soft mound into his face. His nose inhaled the fragrance of her. As she pushed him back on the bed with her hands, he could feel her tongue sliding all the way down his chest and his belly and then feel himself going inside her mouth. He was hard almost as soon as her lips touched him.

Then something was happening. He'd been a little woozy when they'd been drinking in the parlor, but now it seemed to be coming over him again. She was straddling him, and her face kept going in and out of focus. Worse, he couldn't seem to feel himself inside her. His mind felt vague, as if he couldn't concentrate. He took his eyes from her face and tried to fix his gaze on a crack in the ceiling, but he couldn't seem to make the crack stay still. It kept moving.

And then he felt as if the bed were spinning. Spinning and spinning, going faster and faster. Lily Gail's face was just a blur and he felt heavy all over. He tried to speak, but no words would form that he could hear. He could dimly hear them inside his head, but they didn't seem to reach his mouth.

Then it began to grow dimmer and dimmer until everything was like night. The last thought he had was that the sun seemed to be setting awfully early.

It seemed that he dreamed, though parts of the dream seemed so real he actually thought they were happening. The only problem was that he couldn't seem to hear the sound of his own voice or move his arms or legs very well. Everything seemed as if it were swimming in molasses. At some point he knew that he was being lifted up off the bed by strong arms, a man's arms, and that someone, he guessed it was Lily Gail, was jerking his jeans on him. He could see the man dimly, and Lily Gail not quite so well. He kept wanting to ask Lily Gail who it was who had come to their own private party, but the words wouldn't form. After that it seemed like they tried to make him walk, and that made him angry because he didn't want to walk, he wanted to stay in the bed with Lily Gail. But the man was cussing him, calling him a "sonofabitch of a tin badge," something that made him even madder. His damn badge, if it was any of the sonofabitch's business, was made out of nickle silver and had gold engraving on it telling anyone who needed to know that he was a certified, copper-bottomed, steel-plated, one-hundred-percent-guaranteed, original deputy U.S. marshal. And folks hadn't ought to be dragging him out in the night air, especially when he wasn't even wearing his boots. Then he thought he smelled hay, though he knew that couldn't be right because what would Lily Gail be doing with hay in her bedroom? Was she going to keep a horse handy in case she had to leave in a hurry?

There was a bright light, he was almost certain about that. Someone was shining a lantern in his face and he didn't like it, but he couldn't make his arms work well enough to knock it away. Then someone was fooling around with one of his feet. He could feel that he was sitting down and somebody was doing something to his ankle or foot or something. He heard some kind of a clanking noise, and then Lily Gail was giving his some more whiskey so he could make his little soldier stand up and march, and then he didn't remember any more of his dream because it suddenly got dark as the inside of a cow and he felt as if he'd fallen down a deep hole.

Sometime later he seemed to be swimming toward the surface of a deep pond. For a second he broke through the water and was able to breath the free, cleansing air. He knew his eyes were open and that he was looking around, but it was such an effort. He moved and heard a kind of clanking sound. It made him curious, but it was just too much trouble to move around and see where the noise was coming from. He knew he was lying on his back, and he made a slight effort to sit up, but it was still too much trouble. Just before he dozed off again, he smelled hay and wondered about it. But that also seemed as if it wasn't worth the effort of stirring himself around. He lay back and let the black take him.

He came to with a blinding headache and a confused and disoriented mind. It was daylight, judging by the amount of sunshine streaming in through the big doors of the barn he was in. With great effort he slowly sat up, every move sending fresh jolts of pain through his head. As carefully as he could, he looked around to see just

27

where he was. It was a barn indeed, and it was daylight, though by the lay of the sun he could tell it had just gotten good day. It was a big barn, with a hayloft full of baled hay and then a big heap of loose hay taking up one whole side of the barn in a big stack. He blinked his eyes, facing the daylight coming in through the big doors. He could see the doors pulled back and he could see they were painted red.

He looked down at himself. All he was wearing was his jeans. His belt was gone, his gunbelt and revolver, the derringer he had carried in his concave belt buckle, his shirt, his hat, his socks, his boots. He shook his head, trying to remember. It was very difficult, and for a second he was suddenly frightened that some injury might have been done to his head that had knocked the memory clear out of his mind. He wanted to shake his head, to try to clear his senses, but the pounding pain warned him off.

The thought came to him that his mouth was so dry it felt as if his tongue was stuck to the roof of his mouth. He wanted water and he wanted it badly, but he was beginning to feel dizzy. The barn had started to spin around, slowly at first, but going faster with each revolution. He was feeling sick to his stomach, so sick he wanted to throw up. He had glanced at his bare ankle, and vaguely realized that there seemed to be some kind of chain around it. He wondered what a chain was doing on his ankle, but he never got a chance to investigate. The whirling barn got dimmer and dimmer, until he slumped over on his back just as it got completely dark.

The next time he came awake it was to the jolting effects of a bucket of water in his face. He came jerking up, the stabbing, pounding pains going off in all directions in his head, sputtering against the deluge of water.

As he was trying to sit up another wave of water came. But it was partly a blessing because he had his mouth open, gasping for air, and some of the water quenched the dry dust storm behind his lips. Then, whoever it was threw the bucket at him. It hit him in the chest and rolled away. He heard a voice saying, "Wake the hell up, Longarm. You sonofabitch! Git awake 'fore I kick you in the haid an' put you back under!"

He shook his head as best he could, trying to clear it of the water that was still streaming down from his hair and trying to clear the cobwebs inside. As his vision cleared, he saw a tall, rawboned man standing in front of him about five feet away. Beyond the man he saw Lily Gail in the door of the barn, shading her eyes to see into the dimness. The man suddenly walked over and kicked Longarm in the thigh with a hard-tipped boot. "You awake, you murderous bastard? Answer me, boy, 'fore I kick the shit out of you!"

Longarm said, his voice a bare croak, "What the hell is going on?"

"This!" the man said. "You like it?" He kicked Longarm in the same spot on the thigh again. But Longarm's head was hurting so badly he never felt it.

Longarm said, "Who the hell are you?" Then he looked past the man and saw Lily Gail. "Lily Gail, where am I? What's going on?"

The man suddenly kicked him in the chest. He said, "Shut up, you bastard. Don't you be a-talkin' to her. You look at me, you cowshit lawman!"

The kick almost knocked Longarm over on his back, but he partly caught himself with his hand, and then the man reached over and grabbed him by the hair and jerked him forward. "Set up thar! Damn you? You've slept 'nough. You've slept the clock round. Lady here wants you wake enough to 'ppreciate what is a-gonna happen to you."

Longarm looked past the man, seeing Lily Gail. She'd come a little farther into the barn and was standing, her arms crossed, staring at him. Longarm tried to think. Some of the events were starting to come back, but he couldn't figure how he'd come from making love to this delicious young woman to lying in a barn getting the hell kicked out of him by some stranger.

The man stepped back. He looked around at Lily Gail and said, "I reckon he's bright-eyed and bushy-tailed 'nough now. He still ain't a-gonna figure it all out fer a couple hours, but he be pretty ignorant-lookin' to begin with."

Lily Gail said, "I'm much obliged, Emmett. You better git to goin' now."

The rawboned man said, "Yeah, I got a pretty good ride ahead of me. But you shore this the way you want to do it? Hell, I could pack him with me. He wouldn't give *me* no trouble."

She shook her head. "No. I want to see it happen. I want to see him git it."

Emmett looked at Longarm and laughed. "Boy, you is in fer it. Ain't nuthin' quite as mean as a woman when she gits mean, and Lily Gail is feelin' right mean right now." He laughed again. Then he gave Longarm a little salute. "Us will be back in three days, I'd reckon. So I'll see you then. Thet is if she don't skin you alive 'fore then."

He turned around and started out of the barn. Longarm watched as Lily Gail turned and fell in stride with the man. He could just see them as they made their way to where a horse was saddled near the house fence. Longarm watched them exchange a few words, and then the tall man swung into the saddle, gave Lily Gail a wave, and rode out of Longarm's vision. He wondered, crazily, why the man hadn't kissed her. It worried him. At first he had thought that the man was her husband or her lover. But Kyle Greenwood had said she was a widow and that she wouldn't let any of the young bucks come near her.

So who the hell was the rawboned man? And what was going on?

But thinking hurt his head even worse than it was hurting. And his mouth was dry again. The wooden bucket the man had thrown at him was lying by his side. He scooped it up. There was a little water still inside, pooled in a warp in the side of the bucket. He turned the bucket up and drained the last drop, holding the moisture in his parched mouth, letting it bring relief to his tongue and the rest of his mouth, which felt like sandpaper.

He put the bucket down. Lily Gail was walking toward him. There was none of the innocent flirt about her now. Her eyes weren't dancing and inviting. They were set as hard as her mouth. She came to just inside the barn and stopped and stared at him. She didn't speak. He said, "Lily Gail, what in hell is going on?" It came out of his dry throat like a croak. "Give me some water, for God's sake."

She didn't answer him. Without a word she turned on her heel and walked out of his view, heading in the direction of the house.

He was confused, puzzled. Even though his head was pounding and his body craved rest, he forced himself to stay upright and not lay back. If his head would just quit pounding so that he could think! If his memory would just come back, if he could think of any reason why he had come to be in such a state—maybe then he could do something about it.

For one thing he could not remember ever having had a worse hangover. And he didn't remember drinking so very much. He put his hands to his temples and tried to squeeze the pulsating pain into a manageable package. But it kept breaking out around his palms. Hell, he thought, he hadn't had that much whiskey. He'd had a few drinks with Lily Gail while they'd sat on the divan, and then he hadn't drunk anymore after they'd gone into the bedroom. He closed his eyes and squinted up his face, trying to think. They had made love and then she had brought him one more drink.

After that they had . . .

He pressed his fingers to his eyes trying to see what they had done after that. Nothing came. It was a blank. No, wait a minute. She had pushed him back on the bed and gotten on top of him. Then the room had started spinning around.

There was an aftertaste in his mouth. He remembered it from the long drink she'd given him. She'd said it was from the lemonade when he'd remarked that the drink had a different taste, but he didn't think that was so because he'd been drinking whiskey and lemonade before and there hadn't been that kind of bitter taste in the back of his throat. But his mind had been too preoccupied with having her body again.

And had he had her again? He couldn't remember. He could remember her pushing him back and the room starting to spin and then, after that, there was nothing, nothing until now. He did, though, seem to remember coming to in the cold light of morning and wondering about something being over his ankle. What had it been? A chain. He suddenly remembered how sick he'd been, how weak and nauseated.

Now he remembered about the chain and he leaned forward, pulling back the leg of his jeans. There was a chain wrapped around his bare ankle and secured tightly with a small padlock. With a little tremor he grabbed the chain and immediately traced it to its end, to a big roof support only about two feet behind him. That end of the chain was wrapped around the big post and also secured with a padlock. He jerked at the end of the chain around the post. It felt solid. He looked up. The post was made from a solid pine log and rose fifteen or twenty feet into the air to act as one of the three main ridgepole supports for the barn roof. If he moved the post he was going to have to move the barn with it. He guessed the timber to be at least a foot and half in diameter.

He was more than confused now, he was downright flummoxed. And not just a little worried. Was this all part of some kind of plan? Had he just stumbled upon a crazy woman who'd happened to have a crazy man at hand to help her?

And how had he gotten so drunk on so little whiskey that he couldn't remember being removed from the woman's bed and brought out and chained in the barn? He had never been so drunk in all of his life that he couldn't remember in exact detail everything that he'd done or said, sometimes to his acute embarrassment. But this time he'd gone blank for a good many hours, and now he had a head like he'd never felt before. And to top it off, somebody wanted him chained up.

But for what? He tried to think if he'd ever met Lily Gail or the rawboned man before, if they could possibly have anything against him. But his head continued to hurt and his thirst was a torture. He leaned forward and fiddled with the chain around his ankle. It was clear whoever had placed it there had intended that it should stay until they were ready to remove it. The chain was just short of being tight enough to cut off the circulation to his foot, and the padlock was a good sturdy make that wasn't going to be picked with a lady's hairpin. The chain was logging chain with links made up of steel as thick as his little finger. He wasn't going to break one of those or cut them with anything short of a first-class hacksaw blade.

Finally he scooted back and leaned his shoulders up against the post. With one hand he idly played with the chain. It appeared he had about four feet of play in the chain. That and the length of his own body. Ideally, then, he could make a dive at someone if they got within ten feet of him and they were weaker than he was. Though right then that didn't include anyone.

The headache was still there, but it was his thirst that was bothering him the most. He fixed his eyes on the barn door and waited for the moment Lily Gail would appear. Or did she intend to let him slowly die of thirst, torture him with a lack of water as she had first tortured him by withholding her body after practically undressing herself? He shook his head. The lady was a mystery to him. He wasn't scared just yet, but he was getting about as worried as a man can be who is chained in a strange barn by a woman who might be crazy.

He heard a soft nicker and turned his head. In a stall in the back of the barn was his horse. As he watched, the horse dipped his muzzle into a barrel of water and came up, after drinking, slinging water right and left. It made Longarm swallow painfully. They'd fed his horse and watered him. He guessed that meant they weren't altogether crazy, just people with a grudge. He guessed the grudge was against him, though he didn't know exactly why. Maybe they had a grudge against all law officers, or just federal marshals in particular. But even if that was true, it didn't do him any particular good. All it meant was that their grudge was general rather than specific. The results, however, would probably be the same.

After an hour or so, when he thought his aching head could stand it, he began yelling. "Lily Gail! Lily Gail!" He waited for a sound like the banging of a back door being slammed shut behind someone, a footstep, any sound that would signal someone was coming. He waited and listened, but there were no sounds of any kind. He gathered air in his lungs and yelled: "LILY GAIL! LILY GAIL! DAMMIT, LILY GAIL, COME HERE! LILY GAIL!"

He waited. Finally he heard the squeak of a screen door being opened and then the wham as it slammed shut. After a long moment Lily Gail appeared in the door of the barn. She stepped just into the darkness, but kept a good distance between them, at least twenty feet. She said, "What you want?"

He said, "Mainly I want to know what the hell is going on here. But right now I want some water. I'm so dry I ain't got nothing to swallow."

"No" she said shortly.

"No, what?"

"No water. I ain't a-gonna give you nuthin', you sonofabitch."

Longarm stared at her. She had her arms folded just below her breasts. Her eyes sparkled with venom. He didn't think he'd ever seen such naked hatred coming from anyone, man or woman. "Lily Gail, I don't understand what you've got against me. I never saw you before in all my life so far as I know."

35

She spit at him. "Don' you call me Lily Gail, you sonofabitch. I don' let no folks like you call me that. You call me missus. Nuthin' else."

He said, "But you asked me to call you Lily Gail. Don't you remember?" He was talking softly to her, carefully, like you might with a dangerous lunatic. "When we were being nice to each other?"

"Go to hell!" she said angrily. "Don't call it that. It was a trick, you damn fool. Make you trust me. Make you take yore nice whiskey down without tastin' what else was in it."

So it hadn't just been whiskey. That made sense. His mind had lurked around with the idea, but had never come straight out with it. He said, "And what was in my whiskey, Missus Wharton?"

She laughed spitefully. "I guess you'd like to know, wouldn't you?"

"Yes, I would."

She uncrossed her arms long enough to snap her fingers. "That fer what you want to know. Suck eggs first."

He rolled his head around a little, trying to get the last of the cobwebs out. "It must have been something strong, because I can drink a lot of whiskey without it having much of an effect. I knew you was a handful in bed, but I never reckoned you to be smart enough to catch yourself a deputy marshal, Missus Wharton."

She looked at him in disgust. "Quit callin' me Wharton. That ain't no name. That's the name of a town in Texas over near Houston. I wuz just a-usin' it."

"What is your name?"

"That idn't any of yore damn bidness."

"Just like what you put in my whiskey ain't none of my business."

36

"That's right. Mister Smart Aleck Know It All Deputy Marshal Longarm."

"So you know my nickname. You never used it when we were talking or when we were . . ." He let the words trail off and watched her face carefully.

She said violently, "You just go to hell, you ol' bastard."

"You didn't think I was so old when you was using me like a tool."

She almost blushed. "I ain't got time to stand out here and waste it on you. You got yours coming and that's when I'm gonna have my fun."

"Look, I don't know what the hell this is all about. What am I doing here chained to this post? What have you got against me? You know that I am a federal officer. You are buying yourself a big piece of trouble by holding me like this." His brain was still working slow and he knew that he was not handling this woman right, but he didn't know what else to say.

She snapped her fingers again. "That for you bein' a federal officer. Who the hell cares? That badge ain't gonna do you one bit of good when Emmett gets back with yore company."

He stared at her, calculating. He was as lost as he had ever been, in a place and a circumstance that he didn't understand the reason for, and dealing with a woman who must have a hidden side more mysterious than a one-eyed jack. "Well, since you ain't gonna tell me what the hell is going on, the least you can do is get me some water. For some reason you hate me, got something against me. All right. But hell, you'd give water to a dog, wouldn't you?"

She stared at him for a long moment. "A dying dog maybe. Which is what you are only you don't know it."

37

She pointed her finger. "Pitch that bucket over here to me. But you better pitch it mighty easy. You ack like you gonna throw it at me you ain't gettin' nuthin'."

He didn't throw the bucket because it was too much effort. Instead he rolled the wooden pail so that it came to rest at her feet.

She stooped to pick it up. "I don't know how I can work it out to get it to you 'thout you makin' a grab at me."

"Hell, I'll stay back here against the post. You just set it where I can get at it. I don't want no part of you."

She picked up the bucket and was about to start out of the barn when he called out. She stopped just inside the door. "Listen, I got a headache feels like somebody split my skull with an ax. I know you doctored my whiskey with something because I ain't never been hit so hard before. You mind tellin' me what the hell you give me?"

"I done said I ain't gonna tell you."

"Why not? What difference does it make? I just can't figure why I never got on to it."

She leaned toward him and spat the words his way. " 'Cause you had a head full of poontang, that's why. I even put a little in the first few dranks you had and you never taken no notice. All you was interested in was them buttons I was lettin' come undone. And o' course, when I give you the big dose, you'd of drunk down soured milk you was so anxious to get some more of what I'd been a-feedin' you."

"You didn't seem like you was holdin' back your ownself."

"Jest to take you in. You sonofabitch."

"So you put calomel in my whiskey."

"Calomel? Why, you damned fool. I'd of give calomel to a baby. What do I care. I doped you with laudanum.

38

That there last glass of whiskey you put down had more laudanum in it than whiskey." She laughed and put her hand to her crotch. "But all I had to do was shove this up in yore face and you drunk it right down. Which was the last thang you knowed for quite some time."

Laudanum. No wonder his head hurt, he thought. Laudanum was a hell of a strong painkiller. You didn't take it in big doses, and you damn sure didn't take it with whiskey. He was surprised the woman hadn't killed him. He told her so.

For a second it scared her. It surprised him until she told him why. "Oh, my heavens! I'd druther stuck my hand in a hot stove than let you out thet easy! Oh, hell, I wisht I'd of knowed. I was guessin', don't you see. About the amount."

"How much did you give me?"

She looked vague. "Oh, I can't say fer sure. One of them bottles like the doctor gives you. It's been around here ever' since I hoped to fetch you out."

He stared at her. "You gave me one of them whole bottles like the doctor gives out?"

"Not all at once. Just 'bout half of it in that last drink of yores."

"Woman, you are crazy. Listen, you damn fool, I don't know what you and that tramp that liked to kick me in the side so well are playing at, but you better get the key and turn me loose. Kyle Greenwood knows I am out here. You don't go to kidnapping federal marshals. It just ain't done."

"You keep shootin' yore mouth off you'll be doin' it without no water."

"I got a bottle of good whiskey in my saddlebags. I want you to fetch me that. This damn headache is killing me. And I need something to eat."

She stopped and looked back at him. "Fer a dead man you shore want a lot."

"I'm sick at my stomach from that damn laudanum. I need something to eat. And I need a clean drink of whiskey to help my head."

"You'll git what I bring you, sonofabitch!" Then she turned on her heel and disappeared.

He leaned his head back against the big ridgepole and tried to think. He knew he was handling the woman wrong, but he couldn't get his mind in focus. He should have set about bringing her into hand with a single line of questioning. He should have tried to find out what they had planned for him, or who Emmett was and who was he going to fetch, or how could she turn from seductress into a bitch in the blink of an eye, or what she had against him. Instead he'd muddled it all up by asking too many questions about too many matters.

Of course he couldn't really blame himself for that one. He'd known, the moment he'd gotten his eyes opened good, that he'd taken down something that damn sure hadn't agreed with him and it wasn't just whiskey. For all he knew he might have been poisoned, and dammit, he might well have been. The fool woman had given him half a bottle of laudanum, and he was damn lucky to still be alive. He'd remembered, on the few occasions he'd had call to use it—when he'd had some broken ribs and after one particularly painful gunshot wound—how the doctor had cautioned him to use just as little as he could get by with and not to take it with whiskey.

Actually, he reckoned, he was lucky to be alive. All he could do was thank God that his Maker had given him a copper-lined belly and a body that was good enough to keep on operating no matter how badly he treated it.

Of course he realized he was a long way from being out of the woods. Chained securely in a crazy woman's barn was not his idea of safety. But he didn't feel capable of doing anything or any thinking until he could get rid of the irritants of his thirst and his headache. He wondered if she'd even bring him any water. He prayed she'd bring him a little whiskey to help kill his headache, but he wasn't counting on much. He should have played the woman differently, handled her differently. But without knowing what she had against him, he was at a loss as to how to proceed.

And how in hell did this Emmett fit into the picture? And where was he going? He'd said, "Us will be back." Who the hell was "Us"? Or was that just bad grammar?

But all that could wait. He rolled his head back and forth, and opened his mouth and tried to suck some moisture out of the air. Well, at least Billy Vail couldn't see him in the fix he was. He'd always warned Longarm that women or cards would one day be his undoing. At least she hadn't beaten him at cards.

He lay there, slumped against the post, thinking about the woman. Now she could say what she wanted to, but she didn't have to romp with him in bed to get him to drink some whisky watered with laudanum. And even if she'd felt like she'd had to, she'd done a hell of a job for someone who'd just been playacting. If she'd been playacting, then she'd fooled the hell out of him, making him think she was having one hell of a good time. But she didn't have to take him to bed; she didn't have to casually lead him on by unbuttoning her dress. All she had to do, especially if she had that Emmett lurking around, was give him the wallop in the first glass.

41

He thought about the rest of it, and in spite of how bad he felt, it brought a little smile to his face. He didn't know that he'd ever been with a woman who enjoyed it more or let herself go more. She was hot as dynamite and about four times more dangerous.

And he wished like hell that she would come back and at least bring him some water if nothing else.

Chapter 3

It seemed a long, long time before he heard the sounds of her return. He sat up straight, his eyes glued to the door of the barn, anticipating what she might be bringing him. He prayed for water, hoped for whiskey, and had very little prospect of food. But he would take anything she would give him that didn't do him more harm.

She came around the corner of the barn door carrying the bucket of water in one hand by its rope handle and balancing the tray she'd served him whiskey and lemonade on with the other. She came just inside the barn, still some twenty feet from him, and set both the bucket and the tray down. She said, " 'Gainst my better mind I brung you some corn pone and bacon. And the bucket's full of water and you can see the bottle of whiskey."

He said, "Yeah, but it is just out of reach. You just going to leave it there to torment me?"

"I ought to," she said. "But I got a better nature than that. Besides, you'll get yores so bad and so awful, what I can do to you in the meantime wouldn't be shucks. I probably ought to keep you fed up so you will have yore strength up an' kin stand more."

"More of what?"

But she just nodded. "You'll find out soon 'nough. By and by. Was I you I shore wouldn't be in no hurry fer your day of judgment."

While she was talking she'd taken a hay rake from a wall near the front of the barn and was using it to push the tray and the bucket of water within his reach. He started to move forward, but she suddenly jumped back. "You stay right thar', mister, er I'll upset the whole mess and let you lap it off the floor."

He subsided back against the post. "Hell, Lily Gail, I'm tethered up like a bronc on a short rein. My arms would have to stretch six feet to even touch you."

"Well, you just set there an' wait until I'm done and then you kin have it. Don't you move 'fore that."

He watched as she steadily pushed the bucket to where it would be in his reach once he could extend himself to the length of his chain. Then she pushed the tray with the bottle of whiskey. He was relieved to see that it was the brand he had brought with him and that the cork was in and the seal intact. He was relieved, though he couldn't think of any reason why she'd want to dope him up again. That had been done to subdue him and get him chained in the barn. Emmett might be handy at kicking drugged, chained folks, but Longarm didn't reckon he'd wanted any part of a federal marshal, even at the point of a gun.

Longarm didn't know which he wanted first, the food or the water or the whiskey. He figured he'd take a little water first, and then a little food, and then do some serious work on the whiskey in hopes it might cure his head.

Lily Gail said, "Thar. It's mor'n you deserve, but I'd do it fer a dawg. Which is all you are to me."

He looked at her, searching for some clue, some avenue of exploration that might get her to talking, that might reveal some way to win her over before it was too late. He said, "I don't see how you could have done what you done with me and had such a time and been faking it. I ain't gonna claim to know all there is about women, but you shore as hell fooled me."

"That was the genn'el idea. Fool."

He didn't believe her. No woman could fake that. And he'd had a few, for purposes of their own, who'd tried to make him believe they were having a better time than they were. Sometimes he reckoned women did that to make men feel proud of themselves and build up their self-esteem. At least that's what an old, rich whore had once told him, and he'd reckoned she'd known because she'd made a lot of money with that line of playacting.

He said, "Lily Gail, have we ever met up before?"

"What's that to you, Mister Deputy Damn Federal Marshal?"

"Because I'd like to know what I ever done to you to deserve this." He raised his arms to include his state of affairs. "I mean, ain't they a chance you got the wrong fellow?"

"You know any other Custis Longs that is deputy marshals? That work this part of the country killin' folks an' puttin' them in prison? Huh? Do you?"

He frowned at her. "Well, no, but that doesn't answer what I might have done to you. If you could just give me some little idea I might could see the error of my ways. I mean I—"

She gave him a look. "You just set thar and study on it, you sonofabitch."

45

"Wait a minute," he said. "Hey. HEY! HOLD ON A MINUTE!"

But it was too late. She was gone, disappearing out the barn door and turning toward the house. A moment more and he heard the screen door slam as she went in.

He shook his head, and then slowly worked his way over to the bucket of water. It was a good three-quarters full. It was heavy and he was weak, so it was with difficulty that he hunched over and tilted the bucket so he could suck in a little of the water through his parched lips. It was cool and wet and tasted better than anything he'd ever had. He figured he was pretty well dried out by the laudanum and the whiskey, so he didn't want to take in too much. He allowed himself several swallows, and then held a mouthful, swished it around, and finally let it slide down his throat.

After that was the food. The bacon was cold and greasy, but he didn't care. There were six slices, about a quarter of an inch thick, and six pieces of cornbread. He figured to hoard the food because he couldn't be sure when she might let him have some more. But then he couldn't be sure that she might not take it into her head and come and take it away from him.

But to do that she'd have to come within arm's reach of him, and he knew she wasn't going to do that. No, he'd eat one piece of cornbread and one slice of bacon. Then he'd wait an hour and eat some more. All he wanted for the present was to get a little of his strength back and give the whiskey something to rest on.

He ate the bacon and cornbread, chewing slowly and relishing every bite. When he was through he wiped his greasy hands on his jeans, had another sip of water, and then turned his attention to the bottle of whiskey. He picked up the bottle, held it up to the light to see that

46

the color was consistent all the way through, and then broke the seal and worked the cork out with his teeth. After that he smelled the top of the bottle, inhaling the fumes. It certainly smelled like whiskey, he thought. He raised the bottle and took a tentative sip. It tasted all right, and the pounding in his head was begging for relief. He tipped up the bottle and had a hard pull, feeling it going down in his belly and spreading its warmth and untying some of the knots that were buried there. He knew there'd be no immediate relief from his aching head, that the whiskey would take a little time to do its work, so he contented himself with putting down the bottle and eating another piece of corn pone and bacon. The cornbread was gritty and hard to swallow, and the bacon was no less cold and greasy, but he was as glad of it as if it had been an inch-thick T-bone steak cooked just the way he liked it. It was medicine and with every bite, he could feel himself growing stronger as the food drove the nausea out of his stomach. After his second helping of food he drank a little more water, thinking that at least she couldn't ruin that. It was well water, pure and cool, and nothing had tasted as good since he'd last kissed that pretty gal in Denver.

He waited a half hour, wishing he had a smoke, but knowing he might as well wish for a loaded carbine or ice cream. He'd have about as much chance getting either one.

Now that he was feeling better, he began to look around and study his surroundings. The barn, even as new as it looked, did not appear to have had much use. There were bales of hay in the loft at the back end, and there was the big stack of hay along one side just to Longarm's left. It seemed to him to be an awful lot of hay for the few cows he had seen. And why have baled hay and loose hay?

Generally, if a rancher was lucky enough to have his own hay baler, or to catch a baling crew working the section of the country he lived in, he'd have all his hay baled. It was a hell of a lot easier to wagon it out to the cattle on the range when the northers blew in and the grass died and the drinking holes froze over.

The only thing he could think of was that Lily Gail's husband, or whoever had done it, hadn't gotten all of their hay in by the time a baling crew had come by. That was the only explanation for the loose and the baled mixture. Anybody knew that a haystack spoiled from the bottom and it was the worst way to store hay. With baled hay, if it was going to spoil, you'd only lose a bale or two before you moved it around. And besides, Lily Gail's husband hadn't been alive during hay season, so the job must have been done by hired hands.

Longarm tilted his head around to look at the baled hay in the loft. The longer he looked at it the more he began to feel that something was wrong. It was very definitely a much different color, much darker, than the haystack. Now he knew that baled hay did discolor faster, but the hay in the loft just plain looked much older than the haystack, as if the hay had been gathered over different seasons. And that didn't make any sense. As hungry as cattle got, and seeing that they were sold by weight, who'd want to hold out hay and give it a chance to spoil? Longarm shook his head. He was pretty sure that he was not on a working ranch. It might have been at one time, but it wasn't now. It might have been gotten up to look like a ranch in operation, but the only operating that he could see was being done by the lovely little bitch inside the house.

He turned his attention to the ridgepole he was chained to and satisfied himself without much effort that it was solid and wasn't going anywhere. More for the sake of the thing than with any real hope of success, he took one of the links of his chain and tried to dig around the base of the timber with the idea that he might be able to slip the chain under the bottom if he could dig deep enough in the hard-packed dirt. But after a few scratches he recognized that as a fool's game. The ridgepole was set at least several feet in the dirt, and even if he could dig down to the bottom, the weight of the timber would just keep bearing down.

After that he examined the chain link by link, looking for any signs of weakness. There were none. And neither of the padlocks offered much hope. He was caught, whether he liked it or not, and there was no escape, not with the tools he had at hand. He was going to have to find some weakness in his captors and exploit it. But just exactly what that would be, he had no idea.

He used most of the day slowly getting his strength back. He ate again, and had some more water and a little whiskey. The headache was beginning to abate, and he didn't know of anything that felt quite as good as the absence of pain. He took one more drink, and then firmly rammed the cork home. He had the feeling the whiskey was going to have to last him through more than one night, and he'd better space it out unless he wanted to get by with none. He put his head back against the post and let his mind wander around, contemplating the situation.

He wasn't afraid, not particularly, even though it had been made fairly clear to him that there were some people who had some unpleasant prospects in store for him in the not too distant future. Mainly he was curious,

curious as to what it was all about and who was behind it and why Lily Gail had spread around such an abundance of honey to catch such a small fly as himself. Hell, looking like she did, she could just as easily have used vinegar and still have caught his particular fly.

He thought about her for a time, listening to the sound of her voice in his head. She cussed him, but there didn't seem to be any real conviction behind the words. She claimed to despise him and hope the worst for him, but there didn't seem to be any real rage or hate in her. It seemed to him, on reflection, that she was doing something that was expected of her—though by whom, he didn't know—rather than out of personal venom. She hadn't even told him what she had against him. If it was enough to get him chained up in a barn waiting for God only knows what, then it seemed to him she'd have spat out her grievance at the first opportunity. No, he thought, he could be wrong, but it seemed to him as if she was playing out a part. Thinking of it made him feel that the real Lily Gail was the one that had gone to bed with him, that had called him into the bedroom, waiting for him there, ready. She just didn't seem to have her heart in this business of hating him and wanting some sort of terrible vengeance wreaked on him for something he couldn't even remember.

Behind him he heard his horse stamping his foot. He looked around. The horse was standing there, the big U.S. brand on his flank identifying him as a cavalry horse, looking bored. Well, Longarm thought, he wasn't the only one. Now that Longarm was feeling nearly alive, he was beginning to fidget within his confinement. He ate a little more and had another drink of water. He wasn't sure that he'd be brought any supper, so he was saving some of the cornbread and bacon for the night.

The day passed. In the afternoon he got up and walked around as best he could considering his chain. He was surprised how stiff and sore he was. He felt like someone had been beating on him with heavy sticks. The marks Lily Gail had left on him had scabbed over. Lord, he thought, when that girl got passionate she got passionate. He didn't believe he'd ever been with a woman who released herself with such abandon. He let his mind wander back about twenty-four hours, thinking of the way they'd made love. He could feel himself beginning to be aroused by the memory and the mental images of Lily Gail. He immediately shut down that line of daydreaming as dangerous and frustrating.

Finally he just sat down and waited for the day to pass. He thought of yelling for Lily Gail, but he didn't think it would do any good. Once or twice he thought he smelled wood smoke, and he guessed that maybe it was coming from her cookstove, because there wasn't any other reason he could think of for building a fire on such a day. He wondered what she was cooking and if she was going to give him any of it. He was hungry again.

The shadows were beginning to lengthen outside the barn door when he finally heard the screen door bang. He waited, hoping she was coming his way even if it was just to cuss him some more. He'd put a lot of men in prison, and he reckoned that some of them, mean as they were, had eventually ended up in solitary confinement. But after just one day of it, he was damned if he knew how they stood it. He'd never been confined before in his life, and he was rapidly discovering he had no taste for it. So he was hungering for the company of the woman on any terms. Hell, he didn't care if she was coming to threaten him with a gun. Any change would be for the better.

51

After a moment had passed she appeared in the door of the barn, advanced a few feet, and stopped. He could see her blinking as her eyes adjusted to the dim light of the barn. She held out her hand. "Throw me that there tray I brung you earlier."

He still had some cornbread and bacon left on the plate, and he wasn't willing to surrender that. The tray was behind him, beside the post. He turned, slid the plate off onto the ground, and held the tray out. He smiled. "Here it is."

She gave him a look. "Throw the damn thing, fool."

He looked her over critically. She'd changed her gown. She was wearing blue, but it was very like the yellow frock she'd worn the day before. It fit her snugly about her small waist, caught the flare of her hips, and had the same square, low-cut, lace-lined neckline that just revealed the beginning of her cleavage. He noticed that she'd brushed her hair and put on some rouge, though it was difficult to see at the distance with the light being what it was. He said, "Lily Gail, why don't we cut this foolishness out and you come over and turn me loose and we'll pick up where we left off."

She said, "Huh! I guess a stray cat can dream. That's all you be a-doin'."

"You expecting company?"

"If I was it wouldn't be none of yore damn business." Then she stared at him. "What makes you ask such a question?"

He gestured. "Well, you appear to have got yourself all gussied up for somebody. I know it can't be me. So I figured, what with Emmett gone and all, that you was kind of slipping around on the sly."

Her face flamed. She said, "Why you crazy . . . Emmett ain't got aught to do with me. He's just part-time hired

52

help 'round here. An' he don' even work fer me. So you kin just keep them kind of thoughts to yoreself! Now, you gonna sling that tray over to me or not? Or maybe you don't want no supper."

He flicked his wrist and sailed the tin tray across the space so that it landed at her feet. As she leaned over to pick it up and her neckline fell open, he said, "They are still as pretty as ever, I see."

She suddenly straightened up and stamped her foot. "How dare you, you low-down cur!"

He said, "You showed them. I looked. Did you think I wouldn't?"

She bent quickly, grabbed up the tray, and turned for the house. "I think you just lost yore supper."

He called after her. "It was worth it."

She gave him a backward glance and disappeared. He let out a laugh, even though he really didn't feel like laughing. With the dusk coming, and coming faster in the barn, he said softly, "Custis, if you ever played a fish you better play this one, because she's the only chance you got."

It was an hour before she came out again. She came bearing the tray with a big steaming bowl of something on it. There was also a small coffeepot and a big white mug. Longarm had never expected coffee. It made his spirits rise and gave him new hope. She appeared to be softening. He greeted her with a big smile. "Lily Gail, I'm hurt you took what I said amiss."

She said, "You are a-gonna be hurt, but it won't be you doin' the hurtin'."

He saw she was wearing an apron that tied at the waist. On her right side he could see a pocket, and as she set the tray on the hay-littered barn floor he was almost certain he heard something jingle. She's carrying

53

the keys, he thought. She's got the keys in her apron pocket.

But none of that showed in his face. He watched as she took up the wooden hay rake and began to slide the tray toward him. The hay rake was long-handled, as a hay rake has to be if it is to reach the top of a stack or sweep up freshly mown hay. Longarm guessed the handle to be about twelve feet long. The head of the rake, which was a solid piece of wood about one inch thick by two inches high, was at least four feet long. Its teeth were wooden dowels set a few inches apart, and were at least six inches long. Lily Gail had the rake turned upside down, with the teeth pointing up to use the solid part of the head to push the little tin tray. She had to push it carefully through the hay lest the hay get up on the tray and get into his food. He could see she'd put several big biscuits beside the bowl.

He said, "That smells mighty good, whatever it is."

"It's beef stew," she said. "Got onions and potaters in it, but I had to use canned tomaters. Didn't have none fresh."

He inched himself away from the post about two and a half feet, deliberately making it seem as if that was the extent of his reach. He knew she couldn't see the loose chain behind him, covered as it was by straw. As if to help, he stretched out his hand toward the slowly advancing tray. She said, "You just stay back there, you."

"Lily Gail, for the life of me I can't figure what you got against me so hard. I know I could never do any woman looks as good as you and is as sweet as you any harm."

She said grimly, "I reckon you'll find out in due course."

The tray was within his reach, and he grasped its raised edge and pulled it toward him.

"Take yore dishes off there and sling me back that tray. And careful how you throw it."

He skimmed the tray back to her as he'd done before. As she bent to pick it up he again heard the little jingle coming from her apron pocket. He looked into the bowl. It was indeed beef stew. There was a big spoon in it, but no other utensils. He still had the plate from the morning behind him. He said, "This looks mighty good, Lily Gail. Course, not as good as what I can see of you in my mind's eye."

She blushed faintly. "You better shut that mind's eye. You won't be seeing that again."

"What can it hurt to tell me why you are on such a tear against me? At least tell me if it's me or just lawmen in general."

She hesitated, thinking. Finally she said, "I ain't got no love fer lawmen as a bunch, but that ain't it. It's you, you sonofabitch." But she said the last with much less vigor than even the first few times she'd cussed him, which he hadn't thought forceful at all.

"I don't see what it can hurt to tell me. God knows I ain't going anywhere, not chained to this barn like I am. What could it hurt you? Maybe I'd understand."

She stared at him. She didn't speak, but neither did she leave. She put her hands in her apron pocket and jingled around whatever was in there. It wasn't coins, he was sure of that. It sounded like keys if he'd ever heard keys being jangled in a pocket. His hand ached to reach out and grab her. The only problem was that his arm wasn't ten feet long.

He said urgently, "Hell, Lily Gail, it won't hurt you. At least give me that little bit. I'm waiting here scared to death of what I got coming, whoever Emmett is bringing. I'm chained up. For all I know I may never get loose. You ain't a mean woman. I know that from what we did. Give me this little thing."

She looked at him with interest. "You scairt?"

"Hell, yes!" he lied. "Hadn't I ought to be? What chance have I got to make any kind of fight for my own life? None, that's what. And it was you captured me."

She shook her head. "Lordie, I never thought I'd heard the famous Deputy Marshal Longarm say he was scairt. You ain't supposed to be scairt of nothin'. You the one supposed to be doin' the scarin'. Ain't that the way it genn'lly goes?"

"Yes," he said. "But you can see the fix I'm in. What would you reckon? that I'd be havin' a good time? What can it cost you to tell me how come you to trap me like that?" He gave her a slow, appreciative look. "It took some kind of bait to distract my mind like you done. I got to hand you that. So I figure you got a powerful reason."

She said, "Well . . ."

"It couldn't hurt."

She sighed. "I guess not. I'll tell you, but it won't do you no good. And if I tell you, I don't want you sayin' nothin' or makin' no fun. You understan'?"

"Of course, of course. I promise." He could hear the words that had been coming out of his mouth, hear them as he used them like weapons. His mouth and his attitude and his persuasion were the only weapons he had. Somehow he had to talk this woman around to his side. He gave her a solemn look. "Lily Gail, I can't imagine that anything you've felt strong enough about to kidnap a federal officer would be anything to laugh at. And I mean that from the bottom of my heart." And he thought: You don't know how strong I mean it, you crazy bitch. But if I ever get loose from this chain you are going to find out.

"Well," she said primly, "I done it because you kilt my husband and put my cousin in prison."

He stared at her for a moment, a little taken aback, a little off balance. He didn't know what he'd expected her grievance against him to be, but he hadn't expected anything quite so stark. To stall for maneuvering time he said, "You sure it was me killed your husband?"

"Sure as the sun is shining." She stood there, not a flicker of expression on her face.

"Well, how can you be so sure? Who was your husband? And why did I kill him?"

"Bob Drago was my husband. An' you shot him in Ouchita Mountains. Shot him off his horse. Was half a dozen saw you do it and recognized you."

With a sinking feeling Longarm suddenly realized she was right. He recognized the moment and the scene instantly. It had been during the sweep the army had made, trying to box the Gallagher gang in. One part of the gang had split off, and Longarm and a mixed group of soldiers and lawmen had given chase after them up a canyon. A trailing man had stopped and turned to fire delaying cover. With bullets whistling all around him Longarm had stood up in his stirrups, aimed carefully through the sights of his carbine, and shot the man out of the saddle. He had indeed been Bob Drago, a half brother to the Gallaghers on his mother's side, and as mean and cruel and no-account as a murdering thief could be. Yes, he had shot and killed Bob Drago, and up to that second he'd been very glad. Now he was feeling mixed emotions. Then he suddenly said, "But wait a minute! Bob Drago was an outlaw, a mean, low-down sonofabitch. Hell, he rode with the Gallaghers. Are you sure we are talking about the same Bob Drago? You couldn't have been married to *that* Bob Drago, a woman like you."

She nodded solemnly. "That's the one. An' I'm related by marriage to the Gallaghers. They be my kin."

It burst out of him because he didn't want it to be so. "Like hell! You can't still be kin to somebody by marriage when your husband is dead. You ain't no more kin to the Gallaghers than I am."

"They done right by me," she said. "They've seen to it that I've been fixed up. They bought this here ranch. Jest like they own a bunch of other little spreads like it."

He sat very still. "Yeah, so they can disband and go to acting like ranch hands. No wonder we never catch them. They disappear into the countryside. We should have been looking for ranches with ranch hands but no cattle. Like this one."

She gave him a little smile. "You shore are smart. Too bad it won't do you a damn bit of good."

He shook his head slowly. "Lily Gail, ain't nothing but trouble can come from you being mixed up with the Gallaghers. They are going to come to a bad end. I promise you that. You don't want to go down with them."

She smiled even bigger. "Oh, I'll be going along my way after they get here. They are going to give me a great big chunk of money fer catchin' you. Yessir, a great big chunk."

He guessed he was stupid because it was just now beginning to dawn on him. He said, almost disbelieving, "You are not telling me that you set out to trap me for the Gallaghers?"

She giggled. "Yeah, ain't that funny? Course, they been layin' fer you for some time and had other traps out.

But when I heered you was in the neighborhood, Emmett rode to find them and seen what they wanted to do. They knowed you was partial to a little gash, so they set me up to leave word around for you. Sent me right here and said jest to set and wait. And now look what I caught me." She pointed a finger at Longarm. "You. An' not with no gun neither. Jest a little whiskey and a little kitty fur."

Billy Vail's words came back unbidden. Hell, his reputation even extended to his enemies. Was he that predictable? He found his voice and said, "Lily Gail, you are not telling me that the Gallaghers are coming here for me?"

She nodded and giggled and pointed her finger at him. "Yessir. Jest for you. Jest a couple more days."

He said "Sonofabitch!" in spite of himself. Then he gave her a hard look. "Listen, missus, something you better know. You don't kill a federal officer and get away with it. The reason you don't want to kill a federal officer is because every other federal officer in the country will make it his business to hunt you down. We do that because our work is dangerous and we've made it clear in the past that killing a federal officer is about as dangerous a work as you can take on."

She shook her head at him. "Ain't got aught to do with me. I ain't gonna be the one kills you."

"But you'll be an accessory and that is the same thing."

A shadow flickered across her face. "What's that, that 'cessory thing?"

"A helper. It means you were part of getting me killed, that you took part, that you helped."

She shook her head violently. "I never done nothing. I just made a little good times with you and give you a little laudanum and whiskey. Was you that drank it. I never made you. An' I won't be here when the Gallaghers do what they gonna do to you." She suddenly gave him a look. "I'll tell you this fer nothin': They don' like you one damn bit. I heered Rufus call you the worst sonofabitch he'd ever had truck with. I ain't never heered nobody get as good a cussin' as they give you ever' time yore name come up."

He sat there, thinking that Kyle Greenwood had been right when he'd said Missus Wharton knew something about the Gallaghers. As far as Longarm was concerned, she knew a hell of a lot more than he wanted her to. He said, still trying to get his point across, "Lily Gail, it won't matter if you're not on the spot when the Gallaghers take me in hand and do what they've got a mind to. You could be in Mexico, it wouldn't matter. You'd still be a part of it, a helper. Sheriff Greenwood knows I came out here, he knows what you look like, he knows about you. They'll hunt you down no matter where you run. I promise you that."

She looked uncertain for a second, but then her face cleared. "Aw, you are just sayin' that to git me to let you go, tryin' to save yore skin. An' I can't say I blame you. An' I might have been willin' to listen if it had only been that mean sonofabitch Bob Drago. But it was my, my cousin. . . ." Her face suddenly pinched up and she looked as if she were going to cry. He thought he saw her lip tremble.

"Your cousin?"

"Yes. Eugene Swope." And then she almost did cry, but with an effort she righted her face.

"Eugene Swope? Your cousin?"

"Yes," she said. She suddenly looked at him fiercely. "And you sent him to prison. And him so young."

"I don't seem to recall any Eugene Swope."

60

"You know damn good and well who I mean. A tall, handsome man. Fair. And kindly."

He ran the name and the description back and forth in his mind, and then a face began to emerge. At the beginning of the cavalry's pursuit of the Gallagher gang, Longarm and another lawman had surprised three men holding a small remuda in the foothills of the Ouchita Mountains. They'd had them in a small valley that provided a natural enclosure for the horses on three sides. It had also enclosed the three horse herders. One of the men had been a young man of twenty four or twenty five. He'd been blond and fair-skinned, though he didn't fit the name of handsome that Lily Gail had given him. They had been part of the Gallagher gang; a small part, but nevertheless a part. Most of the horses were stolen, so the three men had gone to prison on that charge. Longarm himself had jailed the fair one, who, now that he recalled, had been named Eugene. He'd taken him into Lawton, the same Lawton he was headed for. The other two had been taken off by the other lawmen. He'd never known until the moment Lily Gail had told him what had become of the young man. He said, "Hell, Lily Gail, he was caught red-handed with a herd of stolen horses. What did you want me to do, give him a reward? Hell, it was my job. Are you going to hold me responsible for doing my job?"

She flared at him. "Maybe I don't care for your line of work, *Mister* Deputy Marshal Longarm."

Something was strange here, he thought. "You are telling me that you are more mad at me for putting your cousin in jail than for killing your husband?"

She said sarcastically, "Well, he was kin, after all."

"Look," Longarm said, raising his hands in a kind of plea for understanding. "In the first place, wasn't me put your cousin in prison. That was a judge and jury. And I didn't arrest him all by my lonesome. They was several of us. It just worked out that it was me carried him in to the county jail in Lawton. I just *happened* to be going that way. Could have been another fellow just as easy."

"But it was you!" she said, stabbing her finger at him. "You!" Without being conscious of it she had taken a step each time she stabbed out her finger. She was within a yard or two of his grasp. He tensed himself to spring forward.

But she seemed to realize her danger at almost the same instant he saw the opportunity. She looked down at the floor, and then quickly took several steps back. She stood there, staring at him, her chest heaving slightly.

He said slowly, "Sounds like you and ol' Eugene was close." He said it wondering if he could get her so angry, as angry as she had been when she'd been stabbing him with her finger, that she'd maybe get close enough to try to hit him. "Killing your husband was one thing, but locking up your cousin was another. Maybe you was way yonder more than kissing cousins."

Her eyes flared. "You watch that mouth of yores!"

"Ol' Eugene teach you all them tricks you know about in bed?"

She glared at him, her mouth working but no words coming out.

"That business with your tongue. He teach you that?" She stared at him.

"I bet ya'll started early. Same age? I reckon he must have never even give you a chance to be a virgin. You got to get beyond the age of twelve untouched to ever call yourself a fresh flower."

She suddenly screamed at him, "Shut yore lyin' mouth!" Then she turned around and ran out of the barn. Longarm shrugged philosophically. His tactic had had the opposite effect than the one he'd wanted. But at least he had found out what she had against him, had found out exactly. He looked down. The bowl of stew was right in front of him, as were the biscuits and the coffee. He poured himself out a full measure in the thick mug. But he had talked too long. The coffee was no longer hot. He shrugged, and picked up a biscuit and began eating it, staring off into space, thinking, wondering what advice Billy Vail would have to give. Likely the old bastard would say, "You'd of kept your britches buttoned, it wouldn't have never happened in the first place. I always say a man can't take his pants off an' get in no trouble so long as he keeps his gunbelt buckled tight."

It made him smile. Billy Vail. The old rooster. He might sit behind a desk now with his hair looking like the top of a mountain in winter and his little potbelly he kept trying to hide, but there had been a day when Billy Vail had as round a set of heels as ever got issued. If he'd been shot every time he got in the chicken yard, he'd have been more full of holes than a colander. And Vail had also gotten in trouble with his gunbelt. He might preach caution now, but it was that same Billy Vail who'd once taken the reins between his teeth to free his hands for two guns and ridden straight into a Comanchero camp shooting at everything that moved.

Longarm let out a sigh. About the only thing he could say about Billy was that this was one occasion he wished he and the old war-horse could trade places. Hell, as far as that went, he was willing to trade places with anybody. At least Billy was older and might not mind going so bad. Or maybe they'd take pity on him. Of course Billy would never have gotten in the mess in the first place because Missus Lily Gail's charms would have been wasted on him now.

Longarm tried some of the stew and was surprised to find it very good. Well, that was one thing he could do. He could eat and get his strength built back up. He had a feeling he was going to need it. There was one thing for sure the Gallaghers could count on if they came for him. They'd be a hell of a lot better off shooting him at long distance with a rifle. If one of them got close enough to lay a hand on him, that one would have a broken neck right quick.

Outside it was growing dark. It was already so dark in the barn he couldn't see his bowl of stew. It was going to be a long night. With the help of the laudanum he'd had enough sleep to last him a week. So he figured to be sitting up, fretting. A long night, and him without a smoke and damn little whiskey.

He thought of Lily Gail. She could make the night pass pretty quick if she was a mind to, but he didn't think she would. He sighed. He'd tried getting her angry and that hadn't worked. Somehow, some way, he was going to have to figure a way to get her into grabbing distance when she was wearing that apron with the keys in the deep pocket.

He finished up his stew and biscuits and set the bowl and the coffeepot and mug by the plate, which still had a little cornbread and bacon drying on its surface. After that he had a carefully calculated drink of whiskey, and then lay back on the hard floor, putting his hands under his head for a pillow.

Chapter 4

She came back sometime after midnight. Longarm couldn't be sure because they'd taken his watch, but he judged the time as being that by the look of the sky he could see through the barn door.

She came with a lantern and called his name softly. He didn't think he'd been asleep, but he must have been dozing because he had the feeling that he'd heard himself being called a couple of times before it had finally gotten his attention. He turned and raised up and there she was, just inside the barn door, holding a kerosene lantern up about chest high.

He could clearly see that she wasn't wearing any clothes. She said, "Custis. Custis Long. Wake up. I got something I want to show you." She held the lantern higher so that its glow almost reached to where he was by the ridgepole.

He sat up. He could see her clearly, see the uptilt of her breasts, the slight rise of her belly, the very light brown thatch between her legs. He could feel the heat rising in him like a stove being stoked. He said, "What the hell are you playing at now?"

She took a few steps forward, coming closer to him so that he could see more clearly. She said, using her free hand to lift first one of her breasts and then the other, "I bet you'd like some, wouldn't you?"

He didn't say anything. His mouth was all of a sudden very dry and he could feel the pulse beating in his temples.

She took another step forward. "Can you see it real good?" She thrust her pelvis forward, shifting her feet out as she did so that her legs were spread. "This what you want? Huh? Jest tell me it is." She began to rhythmically pump her pelvis back and forth.

"I'm—I'm not looking," he said, staring at her.

She took another step forward and set the lantern on the floor so that the light shone up, exposing her body just to her neck. It was like a milky white beauty in front of him that he could give any face he wanted to. She said, "Now watch this real close."

She spread her legs and then reached down with both hands, fingering her way through the silken hair and parting the lips of her vagina. "Look here at this. Ain't that what you want? I bet it is."

Even with his own breathing roaring in his ears, he thought he could hear her breaths quicken. He said, "I ain't looking. I got my head turned. It ain't working."

"You looking close? It's all nice an' pink, ain't it? Eugene used to say it looked like the way a steak ought to be cooked. That what you reckon? It be gettin' all wet and warm. I bet you'd like to play with it, wouldn't you?"

His temper suddenly snapped. "Goddammit! Get on outta here, Lily Gail! This is the meanest damn thing

66

anybody ever done to me. Yeah, now I believe you are with the Gallaghers. You are a mean low-life bitch! Get on away from me. You ain't tormenting me no more!"

She said angrily, "Then you oughtn't to have said them thangs about Eugene like you done! You are jest gettin' what you got comin' "

"Get out of here, you damn whore. I bet you've taken to bed every pair of pants come within ten yards of you. You and your precious Eugene. How many he have to share you with?"

She was violently furious. She jerked up the lamp and took a step toward him, holding the lamp aloft. "You shut your mouth, you hear? Don't you dare talk to me like that! I'm a great mind to fling this coal-oil lantern at you and set this here barn on fahr and then watch you burn!"

She was almost within reach again. The bulge in his jeans had subsided enough so that he could think. "Then why don't you do it? But you better be careful. You might not hit me, might not get me doused down with that kerosene. Of course, what could I expect from a whore like you."

"You daren't say that!" she cried. She stamped her foot.

"Not say it?" He laughed. "Hell, Lily Gail, if you had as many ramrods sticking out of you as you've had stuck in you, you'd look like a porcupine."

Her voice was almost hysterical. "You be askin' fer it. I ain't accountable you keep up that line of talk."

"Hell," he said recklessly, "throw the lantern on the haystack. That would be sure to burn the barn down."

For some reason the words caused her to hesitate. He could almost see her calm down. She glanced quickly at the haystack, and then she began backing away. She said, "You're the meanest man I ever knowed. You are just awful!" Then she suddenly burst into tears and ran out of the barn. He could hear her sobbing even after she was out of sight.

He stared after her for a moment, dumbfounded. What had he said to make her suddenly change? He glanced at the haystack, but now, with the lantern gone, it was too dark to see anything. He slowly lay back, pondering the change in her. She was a strange woman, girl really, and no mistake. She was, he decided for the tenth time, as desirable a woman as he'd ever run across. He'd seen better-looking women and he'd seen women with better figures. But there was just something about her, some little something that affected him below the belt like no other woman ever had. She just seemed like she was put on earth as an example for a man to lust after.

He awoke shortly before dawn and sat up, a little stiff and sore, and leaned back against the post he was beginning to know so well. For a while he sat there yawning and wishing he had a smoke and a hot cup of coffee. But since he had neither, he had a long drink of water and then a short pull on his diminishing supply of whiskey. There were two pieces of the stale cornbread left, and he ate those, having to wash them down with liberal drinks from the bucket. There were a couple of slices of bacon left too, but he didn't figure he was hungry enough, or ever likely to be so, to try them.

He sat there trying to think his way out of his predicament. A day had passed, and Emmett was well on his way to wherever he was going. He wondered how far off the Gallaghers were. In Oklahoma City? Tulsa? Broken Bow? Hell, he thought, they could be anywhere, lying low, spending the money they'd reaped from previous robberies. They'd been on vacation for quite a while, six months just about. He wondered how long they could go before the itch overtook them again. Maybe he'd be the spark. Maybe coming down and doing in a federal officer would whet their appetite and they'd take off on another one of their robbing and pillaging raids. And did they cut a swath! Hell, he'd never seen Quantrill's work at the end of the Civil War—too young—but he'd heard plenty about it, and he couldn't see where the Gallaghers were far behind, except they weren't trying to hide behind a flag and a cause. They were just out and out bandits and ruffians and murderers. He wondered what they had in mind for him. If what Lily Gail had said was true, that they had a real hate on for him, he didn't reckon they'd be content with a bullet through his head.

Well, he thought, they didn't have their bird in hand yet. Though he was damned if he knew how the bird was going to escape.

Finally, he had to think about Lily Gail. Recognizing her as his only hope, he'd still managed to go ahead and anger her about as well as anybody could be angered. He grimaced as he thought about the remark he'd made about a porcupine. "Real smart, Custis," he said aloud. "That was just real smart. You plain and simple outdone yourself on that one."

But she'd made him so angry he hadn't been able to hold his temper in check. Normally he could handle his moods when the stakes were high enough, and certainly with his life at stake, that ought to have been reason enough to take great care in his handling of the woman. But dammit, nobody had ever come at him like that. She'd come at him on purpose, tormenting him, teasing him, frustrating him. He couldn't think of anything much

69

crueler to do to a man who was chained up and waiting to die than what she had done.

He sighed and watched as it grew light outside. It didn't much matter anymore. He'd split that blanket good and proper. He'd ruined any chance he might have had of talking her around or maneuvering her into a position to help him, even unwillingly. Now he'd be lucky if she didn't let him die of thirst before the Gallaghers could kill him. It wasn't enough he'd made fun of her precious Eugene. He'd gone and called her a whore and just about everything else he could think of to get on her bad side.

He hated to admit it, but the damn woman had gotten under his skin. He didn't fancy himself a ladies' man, but he'd always been able to hold his own ground where the fairer sex was concerned, giving as good as he got. But this little country girl with her bedroom ways had bedazzled and bedeviled him to the point where he couldn't even keep his temper long enough to manipulate her to save his own life. And what would Billy Vail have to say about that one? Probably take out his big gold watch and look at it and say, "Well, you let a woman drag you down about a minute afore I had predicted. I was nearly on time, but I give you credit for havin' a little more sense. Course you never did understand that yore brains lay above your belt and not below."

And this time he would be right.

To distract himself Longarm slid across the floor to the length of his chain, and then stretched out until he could just reach the hay rake. He pulled it to him by the head until he could reach the handle. He reversed it in his grip. It was surprisingly light for as long as it was. Too bad, he thought, that the teeth were wooden. If they were steel it might make a weapon of some kind, though against guns he didn't give it much chance. But still, he experimented with it, thrusting it forward, seeing how well he could maneuver it one-handed. He could control it with one hand, but only if he held the handle close to the middle. To use it to its fullest length he had to take it in both hands at the end.

As he was fooling around with it he happened to glance over at the haystack and remember the look that Lily Gail had cast that way when she was threatening him with the kerosene lantern. He scooted around on his chain tether until he was as far toward the haystack as he could stretch. He reached out with the hay rake, holding it with both hands, and was just able to swipe at the stack at a place about three feet above the barn floor. To his great surprise the teeth went into the hay and then stopped with a clunk. He had hit something solid. There was something in the hay besides hay. Awkwardly he worked the head of the rake back and forth until a little of the hay began to fall away from the side of the stack. He could see something. It looked like a box with printing on it, but he couldn't make it out because it was still mostly covered with hay.

Instinct suddenly made him stop. He was obviously seeing something he wasn't meant to see, something that was hidden. If he made it clear that he had found out, then he would lose whatever advantage he'd gained.

Not that he knew what that was, but at the moment, he was grasping at straws, both literally and figuratively.

He laid the rake down and lay on his belly staring at the haystack, trying to see through the straw at the box it was hiding. Even though he couldn't see the marking on the box very clearly, there was something very familiar about it. He had stared at it for about five minutes when the answer came. "Hell," he said aloud, "that's a case of dynamite."

And it was. Looking at the stack, he could see it was definitely shaped to cover the oblong shapes of wooden boxes. It was a dynamite dump, maybe more than that, he thought. There might be boxes of ammunition in there. He took the hay rake and did what he could to cover up the openings he'd made in the stack. The knowledge of the explosives excited him. He didn't know how useful they might be, but they were another tool, even if he didn't know how to make use of them. If he could get some matches off Lily Gail, maybe he could threaten to blow them all to hell if she didn't release him. But even to his own desperate ears, that sounded like a kind of hollow bluff. By the time he could throw a match on the hay and have it catch fire, and have the fire burn through the wooden boxes to the dynamite, and have the whole thing get hot enough to set off the dynamite, she'd have time to go in the house, get dressed, hitch up a team, and be nearly to town before he and the barn headed toward the heavens. Even Lily Gail wasn't dumb enough to be taken in by that kind of threat.

Besides which, it was highly unlikely that Lily Gail was going to bring him anything, much less tobacco and matches. If she brought him anything it would be a piece of something he didn't want and couldn't eat and wouldn't wear and would need lye soap and water to wash off. He had played the fool the night before and no mistake. What a time to lose his temper, he thought.

But then he'd been carried pretty hard of late and was a little irritable. The hangover from that laudanum and whiskey was enough to unhinge most folks for life.

He finally shuffled back to his position beside the ridgepole and carefully put the hay rake back where it had been, although he took some pains to scatter some straw over it so that it wouldn't be obvious it had been moved. He kept the handle toward him, but pushed it far enough toward the front of the barn so as to have it appear that it was out of his reach.

Then he sat and waited. There was less than a third of the bottle of whiskey left, though he appeared to have plenty of water. What he didn't have was something to eat, and he wished now that he had saved a couple of the biscuits from the night before. He sat and waited, but he waited without much hope; just sat and stared at the empty barn door and listened with his ears for the slam of the screen door.

He was having trouble keeping his mood up. Generally he was pretty much the same in any situation, just sort of calm and at the ready. But always before, he'd had some measure of control over his situation and safety. Now, his fortunes were completely out of his hands. He was trapped, a prisoner, a chained dog who could only jump around at the end of his leash and slobber and bark. He thought of calling to Lily Gail to see if she'd come out. Maybe if she did, he could find a way to apologize. It might not have the slightest chance of success, but at least it would give him something to do. He figured he didn't have much more than twenty four hours before he was going to meet up, at close quarters, with the Gallagher brothers. He'd long yearned to have them before him, but he didn't think the circumstances were going to be those that he would have chosen.

He was not yet afraid, but he was getting worried. There simply seemed to be nothing he could do. He wasn't going to get loose from the chain, not without the key, and Lily Gail had the key. And without being loose from the chain, there wasn't a damn thing he could do. He didn't think he'd ever been more frustrated in his life.

And then, at what he guessed to be somewhere around nine or nine-thirty, he heard the back door slam. He held his breath, hoping it was Lily Gail heading his way. It didn't necessarily have to be her. It could be Emmett with the Gallaghers, though he hadn't heard the sound of any horses. But then he hadn't been listening that close. He felt his breathing quicken as he heard soft footsteps nearing the barn. The hair started to prickle on the back of his neck.

It was Lily Gail. He slowly let out the breath he'd been holding instinctively.

She came in, wearing the same blue frock she'd had on the day before. She didn't look directly at him, but she was carrying a bottle of whiskey in one hand and what appeared to be a clutch of little cigars in the other. She approached without a word to within ten or twelve feet of him, and then stooped down and set the whiskey and the cigars down. He could see they were tied with a little string and included matches. She stood up and said, "If you'll git me yore tray and plate and the coffeepot over here, I'll make you some breakfast. This here is some more whiskey and some cigars. I seen that you smoked when you first come in my house." She paused. "During the nice time."

It took him so off guard that he stammered. He said, "Well, I thank you mighty much. I mean—"

"You kin take that hay rake 'n pull 'em to you. Jest get me yore coffeepot an' that tray right now. Ain't no need to worry 'bout the dishes. I got plenty of them an' they'll be plenty of time to gather 'em up after—" She stopped.

74

He finished for her. "After the Gallaghers get finished with me?"

She was silent, smoothing her apron against her thighs with her plump little hands. She said abruptly, "What I done to you last night was mean. I'm right sorry."

He opened his mouth and closed it and then opened it again. "Lily Gail," he said, stumbling with the words, "that's mighty large of you to take that attitude. I can't say much for some of the words that come out of my mouth."

She seemed to ignore his apology. "Jest throw me that tray an' that tin coffeepot an' I'll make you some breakfast. I was way late gettin' up this mornin'. Don't know what got into me."

He decided that to say nothing was the best course. She was being stiff and shy and formal, and he expected that was the way she wanted it. As gently as he could he pitched the coffeepot and the tray over to her feet. She knelt and picked them up, being careful not to bend over so that her bodice gaped open. Without another word she turned and walked out of the barn. He watched her go, admiring the undulating way she walked.

Once she was out of sight he got busy with the hay rake and carefully pulled the whiskey and the cigars to his side. The extra whiskey was welcome, but the cigars were a godsend, and left him wondering why she'd brought them to him or why she'd even thought of his comfort. In a way it was a bad sign. It meant that she must be expecting the Gallaghers pretty quickly.

But he broke off that line of thinking to bite the end off one of the small cigars she must have found in his shirt and strike a match. When he got it drawing good he took a good inhale, and then sighed contentedly as he blew out a cloud of smoke. After a few more puffs he decided he could afford a drink of whiskey, so he bought himself one out of the opened bottle. As he drank his eyes fell on the hay rake, and a thought suddenly popped into his mind. It was a daring scheme, and if it failed, Lily Gail was going to be angry as hell at him.

He quickly finished his drink, laid his cigar aside, and placed the hay rake where it seemed just out of his reach. But that was deceptive because he was leaving himself a couple of feet of chain to stretch himself out with. And the last time she'd come in, to set down the whiskey and cigars, she'd come within ten feet of him, twelve at the outside. If she did that when she brought his food he might have a shot at her.

The rake was placed, but he picked up hay off the barn floor and did his best to conceal its position. When he was finished he sat back and surveyed his handiwork, picking up his cigar and drawing on it and going over in his mind what had to be done and just how it had to be timed. The important moment would be when she bent over to set the tray on the floor. It was then that he had to act, and he only had a second in which to pick up the rake, use it as a hook, and drag her in before she was aware of her danger. At any point, if he was late or slow, she could escape with a shrug or a sidestep. It was a very chancy play.

But the keys in her apron were prize enough for any risk.

He sat there, waiting. He had positioned himself about two feet from the post with his feet under him, in a kind of squat. He had his arms folded across his knees, but his eyes were on the end of the hay rake and his mind was rehearsing every move that he had to make the lunge for the rake as she bent over, grasping the handle with his left hand foremost and his right hand at the end, picking the rake up, swinging the head in behind her, and then grabbing her with the left side of the head and jerking her to him. It had to be done while she was bending over if he was to be able to give her the impetus to propel her to his grasp.

He could feel his heart beating a little faster and his breath rising sharply. He took a draw off his cigar and then reached over, pulled the cork, and had a quick pull on the bottle of whiskey. Then he carefully extinguished his cigar, being careful not to bend or fray it, and set it and the bottle of whiskey in comparative safety behind the post, where he had the other articles he'd accumulated, including the new bottle of whiskey that Lily Gail had brought him. He expected, if matters went the way he'd planned, that there was going to be a good deal of flailing around, and he didn't want what few cigars he had ruined. He certainly didn't want any bottles of whiskey broken.

He heard the now-familiar sound of the door banging to, and he got up in a kind of crouch and got ready. He was still astounded at her change of heart, her regret about what she'd done to him the night before, but he wasn't going to trust that feeling to extend to letting him go free. She might well be talked around to such a state, but he was beginning to believe that he didn't have that much time. He decided that he had this one chance and he had better make it work. Once he had his hands on the keys there was nothing she could do to stop him, and then he planned to give the Gallaghers as warm a welcome as they'd ever gotten. There'd be no time to send for help, but he didn't think he was going to need any.

Then she was coming through the barn door, walking carefully, her eyes on the tray as if she was carrying something that might spill. He watched her, his eyes narrowed, calculating the distance. Of late she'd been coming closer and closer, and she came on until he figured one more step and she'd be in reach.

She took two more, and then bent to set the tray on the floor as she always did. As she began to straighten up he moved, as fast as or faster than he ever had before in his life. With one swoop he had the hay rake in hand, and with a forward lunge he thrust it out behind her back. Then, with a jerk from his powerful shoulders, he caught her in the small of the back, just as she came erect, with the left arm of the rake's head. He pulled with all his might from a position on his knees. It took her completely by surprise. Her mouth and eyes opened wide and her arms went out, and suddenly she was flying straight toward him. In a motion he dropped the rake and caught her as she crashed against his chest. He let himself go over backward, wrapping his arms around her wildly hitting and flailing hands and trying to lock her legs with his. He could get his right leg over her, but he was at the extent of his chain and he couldn't raise his left leg.

She was screaming something in his ear, and biting and hitting and scratching with a strength and feorcity he didn't think she possessed.

But he cared less for what little pain she was inflicting on him. His one thought was to get his arm free, his left arm, and get his hand inside her apron pocket where he'd distinctly heard the metallic jangling sound as she'd walked into the barn. He gripped her as tightly as he could with his right arm while he slipped his left hand down in between them, searching for her apron pocket.

She was a handful, a surprising handful. All of a sudden she started rolling her body back and forth, trying to break his grip. He was yelling, "Stop it! Stop it! I ain't gonna hurt you!" but she paid him no mind. He considered grabbing a handful of her hair with his left hand while he knocked her out with his right, or perhaps choking her into unconsciousness. But he was so close he thought another second and he'd have the key, and then he could subdue her in a little more gentle fashion, she had, after all, been regretful for the torment she'd put him through the night before.

As his hand searched for the opening to her apron pocket she suddenly fastened her teeth in his bare shoulder. "Damn!" he said. "Quit it, goddammit! I ain't gonna hurt you. Hold still!"

And then his searching fingers found the top of the pocket and, despite of the way she was heaving about, he was able to work his hand inside. In another second he would have the keys.

And then his fingers found metal and identified a knife and a fork and a spoon. The jangling and clanking had been cutlery, cutlery she was bringing for him to eat with. He was so shocked for a second that he just lay still, not doing or saying anything, while she kept on biting his shoulder and fighting him with all her strength.

In an instant he knew he had to save what he could out of the situation. He couldn't let her know that he'd been after the keys. It had to have been done for some other reason, grabbing her like that. There was only one he could think of and only one that she might buy.

He abandoned the apron pocket and jerked his left arm up and grabbed her by the hair and pulled her head back, getting her teeth out of his shoulder. Their faces were so close their noses were touching. He said, "What the hell's the matter with you?"

She screamed in his face, "Let me go! Turn me loose!"

"Not till you kiss me, dammit! All I want is a kiss. I ain't expecting nothing else."

He could see surprise come over her face. Her big green eyes blinked. She said, "What?"

"Kiss me. I want a kiss."

"You want . . . Not till you let me go, you bastard. What is this all about?"

"You should ask after the shape you left me in last night. Hell, feel me down there. Go ahead. Just be damn gentle. They are sore and swollen after the load you pumped in 'em last night with that little act of yours."

He could feel her hand starting to slip between them. He let go his hold of her with his right arm and quickly ran his hand up under her dress, which was already up around her waist. He found smooth, soft skin on the inside of her thigh, and used that to guide himself to where he knew it would be warm and wet. The instant he found the silken hairs and then the soft flesh, he began to get hard. An instant later her hand found him. She felt him, and then raised her head back a little. "You just want a kiss?"

"Yes," he said, lying.

"That's all?"

"Yes," he said, lying again.

"All right. But you got to let go of me."

It really didn't matter. She was no good to him without the key. Maybe this way he could win more of her trust. He took his leg from around hers and spread out his arms. "That letting you go enough?"

For a few seconds she lay atop him, motionless. Then she suddenly pecked him on the mouth and sprang free, seeming to leap off his belly onto her feet. She ran backward a yard or two, stopping just short of where the tray still sat on the barn floor. The hay rake was nearby and she kicked at it with her foot, kicking it out of his immediate grasp. She stood there, staring at him, her bosom heaving. She said shakily, "You scairt the hell out of me."

He sat up. "I'm sorry. I never meant to, Lily Gail. All I wanted was a kiss, but I knew you wouldn't come over here and just give me one. I knew you wouldn't trust me."

She stared at him. "Well, why should I? You're a-waitin' there to git shot. Am I supposed to believe you wouldn't clamp on to me and use me fer some kind of hostage?"

He spread his arms. "Well, did I? Aren't you standing over there out of my reach? Ain't you safe? Didn't I let you go?"

She looked uncertain. "Well, I guess so. I ain't sayin' it is so, but it appears that way."

He was a little irritated with his failure, and it showed in his voice. He said, "Hell, what more proof do you want? My fight is with the Gallaghers, not you. I don't fight with women and I don't use them in my fights."

She put her hand to her breast. "You plumb scared the breath out of me when you whipped me up with that hay rake and jerked me over on you. When yore big ol' arms and laigs wrapped around me I jest near stopped breathin'. I thought I was a goner shore enough."

He looked at his shoulder where her teeth indentations were oozing blood. "You sure didn't fight like you was helpless." He smiled ruefully and felt the fresh scratches on his face and neck. "If I ever get out of this and get another chance with you under better conditions, I'm gonna insist you wear mittens. When you're fighting me you scratch. When you're making love you scratch. Man lived with you a year he'd bleed to death."

Her face softened. "You sayin' you want some more?"

"Of course I want some more. Why do you think I wanted to kiss you? I was going to kiss you and then let you go and hope you'd trust me enough that we could do a whole lot more than just kiss. And by the way, that wasn't very much of a kiss you give me when you took off in such a hurry."

"I didn't believe you."

"Do you believe me now?" His heart was in his throat as he asked the question. If he could just get her to trust him a little bit, he felt sure he could outsmart her in some way.

She put her hand to her bosom again. It appeared to Longarm to be a sort of studied gesture, as if she'd seen some other woman do it and had copied it for effect. In another time and another situation he might have found her amusing. Right then there was nothing in his world he found the slightest bit humorous. She said, "I still don' know what I ought to think."

"Well, you come in this morning and brought me the whiskey and cigars and said you felt bad about them monkeyshines last night. I figured we was kind of trying to make it up."

She got an agonized look on her face. "But don't you see? Ain't no way I can make it up with you. Word has gone out. Emmett has ridden for the Gallaghers. Ain't no way to stop it now. Besides, you put Eugene in prison."

"*I* didn't put Eugene in prison. He did. And a judge did. I just took him to jail. But I *could* do a lot about getting him out of prison if I can get away from here alive."

She stared at him narrowly and with suspicion. "You could?"

"Yes."

"How?"

"He's in a federal prison," he said, lying. "Federal marshals have a great say about prisoners in federal prisons. I could get him out of one to move him to another and just happen to lose him along the way. It has happened before."

He saw interest suddenly blossom in her face, but just as quickly, it died out. "You're jest sayin' that to get me to turn you loose. You wouldn't do that fer Eugene."

"For Eugene, no. For you, yes."

"Aw, you jest be lyin'." She suddenly put her hands over her ears. "I ain't gonna lissen to no more of it."

But he felt like he'd planted some seeds. They didn't have much time to grow, so he felt they'd need considerable watering and fertilizing. "You might at least hand me my breakfast. It's right behind you."

She looked behind her and said, "Oh!" Then she walked around the tray and studied it for a moment. "You've upset yore coffeepot and it's done run all over everything. And yore steak an' eggs is cold. An' the coffee got on yore biscuits."

He said, "Well, why don't you make me some fresh coffee. I don't care if the steak and eggs are cold. Just slide them on over here. Or why don't you act like you trust me and just carry them over to me."

"You'll grab me."

He raised his right hand. "I swear I won't."

She eyed him narrowly for a moment, and then leaned down and picked up the tray. She took three cautious steps toward him and then stopped, just out of his reach unless he lunged. But then he didn't have any reason to lunge because she didn't have the keys. She leaned down and set the tray on the barn floor, picking up the coffeepot as she did. He stared up at her with an innocent expression. "See? I never made a move."

She was about to turn back when she stopped, reached in her apron pocket, and took out a knife and a fork and a spoon. "Oh, I blame near forgot 'bout yore utensils." She bent down and put them on the tray, and then pushed it toward him with the toe of her slipper. "I could warm them steak and eggs up pretty quick."

"No, I don't care, hungry as I am. I would like that coffee right quick, though."

"I never ast. You jest take it black 'er you like cream 'n sugar?"

He smiled. "I like a little sweetenin' in it. Whyn't you just stick your little finger in it for a second."

She blushed and said, "Oh, my! Now would you lissen to him."

He looked up toward the ceiling as she turned and hurried out of the barn with the coffeepot. He was afraid the sky would open and strike him with a thunderbolt if his mouth said many more such things. But he reminded himself that a desperate man is just that, desperate, and shouldn't be held to account like a man in normal circumstances.

She was back before he could really get started on his meal. She said, "They was still some hot in the big pot. I just poured it up out of that." She set the pot down in front of him and, as he turned to get the big mug behind the post, said, "I just put regular old sugar in it. I didn't want to burn my finger."

"Won't taste the same," he said.

She was standing about three yards back from him. He poured a little whiskey in his coffee, and sipped at it slowly while he watched her over the rim. He said,

"I ain't kidding about Eugene. You might think you are going to get some vengeance by turning me over to the Gallaghers, but you would gain a hell of a lot more by letting me go."

She said, her face contorting, "I cain't! Don' you see that? Why, if they thought I'd let you go they'd skin me 'live."

"But you could go with me."

"What about the money? They gonna give me a big chunk of money for you."

"Hell," he said, lying, "I've got quite a bit of money put away. I could give you two thousand dollars."

She shook her head. "You are just makin' all that up. I let you go you'd be outta here quicker'n a cat with his tail on fahr. I've heard sweet talk afore, you know. That damn Bob Drago, butter wouldn't melt in his mouth 'fore we was married. 'N after that wadn't a day didn't go by he didn't beat the thunder out of me. I've heared men talk all my life. And I've seen how they act after'rds. I know all 'bout that. Eugene was the onliest one ever treat me nice after'rds. An' now you done throwed him in prison."

He sighed and poured some more whiskey in his coffee while he chewed a piece of the tough steak. "Lily Gail, I'm gonna tell you one more time that you can't get away with killing a federal officer. I don't care how much money the Gallaghers give you. You can't hide. Look, Sheriff Kyle Greenwood knows where I am. He knows I've come to see you. What you don't know is that I said I'd be back in Wichita Falls today. And that's a fact. Now if I don't show back up there he's going to come looking for me. Now do you want him to find me chained up out there in the barn? It wouldn't look too good for you."

85

She said, staring him straight in the eye, "He already come by, yesterday afternoon. I tol' him you looked in and ast me a few questions and then went on to Lawton. Said you told me in case he inquired."

He stared at her. He was lying about being expected back in Wichita Falls. Was she now lying about Kyle Greenwood? "He come by asking after me?"

"Reckon he got his days mixed up," she said. "He thought you was due back yesterday. I set him straight 'bout you goin' on to Lawton. Said you said something about a prisoner there you had to talk to."

He burst out laughing. "Why you little lying devil! Kyle Greenwood was no more by here than my first wife was! And I ain't never been married. How come you to make up that story?"

She just shrugged and crossed her arms over her breasts. "I just wanted you to know that two could play at that lying game."

He shook his head and pushed his plate away. He had the stump of his cigar at the ready, but he took a moment to extend both his legs. "I'd give five dollars to sit in a chair. This here sittin' on the floor all the time is getting old. Why don't you bring me an old chair. Just a little wooden one. Anything to sit on."

"Why? So you could sling it at me and knock me out?"

He shook his head. "Aw, hell, Lily Gail. I give up. I guess ain't nothing I can say will get you to trust me."

She turned and started for the door of the barn. A few feet from the opening she turned and faced him. "Maybe I do trust you. Just a little bit, anyway."

"Will miracles never cease? What little thing caused that?"

"Well, when you grabbed me with that rake and had me down, I figgered you was after these." She reached deep into her apron pocket and came out with a little ring of keys. She jangled them. "These here."

He stared at the keys. He said, a little hoarsely, "You mean you keep them in your pocket?"

"Oh, shore," she said. "All the time."

He stared, and then he reached over and had a hard drink straight out of the bottle. "All the time?"

She looked innocent. "Yeah. Right here in this big apron pocket."

"How come?"

"So I always know where they are. See, I'm real bad at misplacin' little things. So I got in the habit years ago of puttin' 'em in jest one place an' keepin' 'em there."

Chapter 5

"So you had the keys with you just now. You didn't get 'em when you went back in the house for my coffee?"

She looked at him innocently. "Naw. I tol' you, I allus carry 'em in my apron pocket so's not to mislay 'em. What if the Gallaghers was to come by an' be in a hurry to cart you off an' I couldn't find the keys? What you reckon would happen to me then? Well, I don't know, but I do know I ain't gonna take no chance of findin' out." She patted her deep apron pocket. "So that's why these here keys stays right here. I wear my apron around most of the time so I know what is what, and where is where."

"Yes," he said. He didn't want to say any more. The surprise and disappointment had almost caused him to throw away what little good will he'd built up. But all was not lost. He had her coming near him now. The last time she'd been near him he could have lunged and grabbed her. The thought of the lost opportunity made him almost sick to his stomach. But he had to keep a good face on it. "I shore would appreciate something to sit on. And I need a shovel."

She stared at him. "A shovel. Whatever do you want a shovel for? You can't dig up that post."

He didn't look at her. "Do I have to tell you?"

She blushed slightly. "Oh. All right. They's some old newspapers in the house I'll fetch you."

When she came back she was carrying a short shovel and a cane-bottomed straight-backed wooden chair. She'd tied some newspaper to one of the legs of the chair. She didn't come close, but instead pitched the chair and the shovel near enough that he could reach them. She said, "I'm gonna take me a bath an' change my linen." She fanned herself with her hand. "I jest can't stand bein' all sweaty and not gettin' cleaned up."

He said, "How do you reckon I feel? I don't guess you'd consider bringing me out a bucket of water I could use to wash with and a towel of some kind and maybe a bar of soap. I feel like some of this barn dirt is worked into my skin."

"I seen right away, minute you come in the door, you was a man cared 'bout his appearance. I like that in a man. Now that Bob Drago, that durn animal could go fer months an' if his horse didn't cross a river he never got a bath." She turned for the barn door and then stopped. "Maybe when I get all cleaned up I'll make us a pitcher of lemonade and brang it out here and we kin talk."

He said, with the slightest touch of irony, "That'd be just like old times, wouldn't it? But have we got time?"

She looked vague. "I would reckon. I ain't lookin for Emmett an' them back much 'fore tomorrow afternoon. But I want to get me that bath. You didn't see my bathtub when you was in the house, did you?"

He shook his head slowly. "No, I reckon I missed that one. Is it big?"

"Lord, yes! An' it is tin and covered with enamel on the insides. Got it from that mail-order house, Sears and Rareback. Outta the wish book."

He said, putting a touch of sadness in his voice, "Wish they had a wish book for what I'm wishing right now."

She got a little pained look on her face. She opened her mouth and then closed it and said, "I'll bring you as big as pail of water as I kin find. You don't want it heated, do you?"

"Lord, no!"

"Seems to me I take me a hot bath 'n I get out, I'm all cooler than if I taken a cold bath to start with."

"No, don't take the trouble to heat mine. I'll just take pleasure in cooling off."

Then she was gone, and Longarm sat down in his chair and lit a cigar and stared out the door and shook his head. He was about to come to the conclusion that he'd rather face the Gallaghers with no chance than to keep on making addle-brained talk with Lily Gail. His only consolation was that he was not being overheard, but his own ears were starting to get sick of the soothing lies and manipulations that were coming out of his mouth. But he reckoned there was no end of shame a man would go to to save his own neck.

But there was also the consideration that he was trying, at the same time, to catch the Gallaghers. It wasn't much of an excuse for the way he'd been mealymouthing around, but it was the best he could think of. One thing for damn sure; if the Gallaghers found him unarmed and chained to a post, the odds were damn poor that they would surrender themselves and their arms when he placed them under arrest. And it was too bad that

Lily Gail didn't understand how serious he was being when he warned her about the danger of participating, in any way, in the death of a peace officer, especially a federal officer. That was the one thing he could be sure of. If the Gallaghers succeeded in ending his career and his life, it would probably be the biggest mistake they'd ever made. They had thought they'd been hunted before! Once it was discovered he had died at their hands, and that would be easily be found out by tracing his trail back to Kyle Greenwood, the Gallaghers would be hunted day and night until they were caught or killed.

And Lily Gail right along with them.

She came in then, lugging a ten-gallon pail of water. He got up to go forward to help her, but she set the pail down and retreated quickly before he could reach her. He didn't say anything, just shook his head. She'd left the big pail a foot outside his easy reach, and he had difficulty snagging it by its wire-and-wood carrier and pulling it to himself.

She said, "Well, I'll be a little while. Better'n an hour, I'd think. Then I'll make us that lemonade. And we can have us a nice visit."

"Don't hurry," he said.

When she was gone he looked at the pail of water and the shovel. He had asked for them for the reasons he'd given, but now that he had them he thought it might not hurt to have a go at the ridgepole. He looked up at the ridge spine that ran the length of the barn, the big timber at the top of the roof. It was supported by two posts at each end and the middle one, the one he was anchored to. Maybe, he thought, he could dig out under the post with the help of the water and the shovel, and maybe the middle pole wouldn't sag down to fill up whatever hole he could make as fast as he could make it.

He picked up the heavy pail of water, surprised that Lily Gail could lift it, much less carry it as far as she had, and poured a little on the hard dirt packed around the post. He waited, smoking his cigar, while the water slowly seeped into the hard, red dirt. When it looked damp he poured on a little more and then waited again. This time it took the water longer to seep into the dirt. When the standing water was finally absorbed, he took the shovel and dug a little trench around the post, digging out about six inches from the big timber. Even with the soil dampened, it was hard going. He kept the dirt in one neat little pile so, if he had to, he'd be able to replace it without any sign showing he'd been at work.

When he had a little trench all the way around the post, he poured in some more water. The trench was only a couple of inches deep, so it didn't take a great deal out of the ten-gallon bucket.

He couldn't wait for it all to soak in. He worked feverishly, jabbing the shovel hard into the dirt, which was still rocklike, circling the post, enlarging the trench. Lily Gail had said she wouldn't be back for an hour, but he couldn't take the chance of being interrupted and stopped. Once he'd started he'd begun to get excited about his chances. Just how deep, he thought, could it be to the end of the post? Surely, the post was secured well enough to the roof ridgepole that it wouldn't sag down. If he could just get the hole deep enough and get the ground soft enough, he knew he could work the end of the chain under the post. Then he'd be free. True, he'd still have the chain around his leg, but it was only ten miles to Wichita Falls, and he could make that if he had to crawl on his hands and knees.

He kept working, alternately moistening the ground and then wedging out what he could with the blade of his shovel. He couldn't drive the shovel deep with his foot, as he normally would have, because he was barefoot, so he had to supply all the power with just his shoulders. Within half an hour he was sweaty and hot and discouraged. The deeper he dug the more claylike the soil became. The water wouldn't soak in and consequently soften it, and after digging down better than a foot, there was no sign of the end of the post.

He stopped and stared at it. He'd used up nearly half his bucket of water and it was all for naught. He looked up at the ridgepole in the top of the barn. He was almost positive he could see a little sag in the roof of the barn. If he kept digging the whole barn would end up in the hole. He stepped back, panting. At the end he had been flailing at the hard dirt, trying desperately to find the bottom of the post. He'd gotten carried away with his own enthusiasm. Or his own desperation. He hadn't thought much of the idea when he'd first assessed it, and that initial appraisal had been correct.

Now all he had was a hole and another chance gone. "Hell!" he said aloud. He suddenly looked around. He didn't know how long he'd been working, but he didn't think he had much time left. He began unbuttoning his jeans and pulling them down. At least the damn hole was going to be good for something.

When he was through, he carefully shoveled the loose dirt and clay back into the hole and then patted it down with his shovel. After that he scattered hay around until it covered his work.

Now for certain Lily Gail was his last hope. He rubbed his bewhiskered jaws. There was nothing he could do about that. He doubted she'd trust him with a razor. But he could, at least, have a bath with the water he had left.

He took off his jeans and ran them up the chain so they wouldn't get soaked. Then he stood in the big pail and used the towel to sop up water and get himself wet all over. After that he stepped out of the pail and took the bar of soap and worked up a lather all over his body. When he was finished he picked up the pail and held it over his head and poured about two thirds of the remaining water over him. It felt, he thought, about as good as anything he'd ever felt outside of a mountain stream in Colorado, and God, how he longed for one of those just at that moment.

He finished up his bath by sopping the towel and getting the soap out from under his arms and out of his ears and other places. Finally he flushed himself off with the last of the water, cooling himself off for maybe the last time. Then he wrung the towel out as good as he could and dried himself as best he could, though he knew there wasn't a hell of a lot of reason for it. Within ten minutes he'd be sweating again and dirt would be leaking out of his pores. If Lily Gail was to see him at his best she'd better hurry.

He ran his jeans back down the chain and struggled into them. He'd taken his bath away from his main living area so the ground wasn't too wet. Not that it made much difference. There wasn't much chance to stay neat and clean in his situation. Sometimes he wished he wasn't so fastidious about his cleanliness and appearance. As a deputy marshal he was constantly getting into circumstances that caused him to go days covered with grease and sweat and grime and grit. He vowed, and he supposed he meant it at the moment, that if he ever got out of his present fix, he was going to be a little more choosy about where he went and what he did. Billy Vail could just send some of the younger marshals out on the dirty jobs. He'd earned the right to pick and choose, by God.

But he also knew, even as he made the vow, that he'd never change. He'd take whatever jobs came his way and not give them any more thought than he had before.

He just hoped and prayed that he might get a chance to choose not to choose his future jobs.

When he was all done with everything he sat down in his chair, tipped it back against the post, and lit a cigar and pulled the cork on the new bottle of whiskey Lily Gail had brought him. Taking a drink, he had to admit that his lot had improved since he'd woken up with that godawful headache and a mouth that felt like an alkali flat. Since then he'd been watered and fed and whiskeyed and given a smoke and even a little show. Hell, he didn't have that much to complain about. Things had done nothing but look up.

But what he wouldn't give for his revolver with six cartridges in the wheel. Just six, just a chance, just a fighting chance.

Lily Gail came out about half an hour later. She had changed into a white frock that was shorter than any he'd seen her in before. It was barely ankle-length and had little ruffles around the skirt. It had a V-necked neckline and was buttoned up the front. The top two buttons were undone so that he could see the pink bodice of her camisole. The bodice was also cut low so that her cleavage was clear almost to where her breasts began to swell. He wondered if she was planning on giving him another show.

She came bearing just a wooden chair. She set it carefully on the barn floor, being certain that the hay rake was out of his reach and that she was far enough back where he couldn't reach her even by stretching. Then when she had the chair placed, she said, "Now I'll go get us our lemonade."

He wanted to say, "Don't bother on my account," but he thought it was good politics to let her think she was pleasing him, so he said, "Oh, my, yes. If there is one thing I like better than whiskey, it is whiskey and lemonade. Lots of sugar now, Lily Gail."

"Well, I'll just be a minute. You wait right there."

He almost laughed when she said it because it was said unconsciously, as if she was blind to his plight.

She was back in five minutes, carrying a rickety little table that was topped with a pitcher of lemonade and two glasses. She carried it carefully, watching all three of the objects on its top as if they might suddenly develop legs and jump off the table all on their own. She stopped as she got to her chair, and said, "Now, if you wouldn't mind, Custis, just git behind yore post and I'll set this table kind of between us so's you can reach and he'p yoreself."

He gave her an amused look, but he got up and shuffled around behind the post and put his back to it. He said, "Look here, Lily Gail, I ain't even watching. You could run over here and kiss me in the ear and it would take me so off guard I'd be froze to the spot. Take a noon sun to melt me loose."

She giggled. "You kin come on back round again. It's all set. I poured you a half a glass."

She was back in her chair, a glass of lemonade in her hand and a cardboard fan in her lap. Except for his chain and their whereabouts, it could have been the scene from a couple of days past.

He went to the table, having to stretch and lean against his chained ankle, and got his glass and then went back to his own chair. He poured himself a recklessly strong drink. From the looks of things he was going to be finished before the whiskey was. Besides, he needed something to kill the taste of the lemonade. He raised his glass in a toast. "Luck," he said.

"Luck," she said.

He took a long drink. She did too.

"Well, Lily," he said, "here we are. I must say you look mighty delicious."

She colored slightly. "Well, thank you, sir."

"That supposed to brighten my last hours?"

She said uncomfortably, "I wish you wouldn't talk like that. It ain't fair."

"Fair? You're not talking fair to me, are you, Lily Gail?"

She squirmed in her chair. "You claimed you done what you done about Bob and Eugene on account it was yore job. Well, it's the same for me. Can't you see that?"

He shrugged. "Well, ain't much point in arguing about it, is there? I ain't going to waste no time in disagreement when I can be using my eyes to look at as pretty a woman as I think I've ever seen." He bent slightly forward. "I must say, Lily Gail, you do yourself well on them dainty little things you wear, your small clothes. Is that pink thing silk?"

She didn't blush. Instead she said, primly and proudly, "I allus liked nice soft thangs next to my skin. Eugene used to give me money to buy 'em. Course he went away." She turned her head when she said it, trying, he supposed, not to blame him. "An' then the thangs I had kind of wore out, until Rufus Gallagher set me up here and give me some extra cash. So I got me some nice thangs from that mail-order house, much nicer than you can git around here. An' of course, I got me that tub."

"So this place actually belongs to the Gallaghers?" It was a daring question, but she could either answer it or not.

"Yeah," she said. "I thought you knowed that. Course, it ain't in they own name. They use other folks fer that. But say, I got me a pair of silk stockin's. A real nice pink. You'd like 'em."

He said, "Why don't you unbutton a couple of those buttons on the front of your dress. Let me enjoy a little more of the view."

"I thought that made you mad. It did the other night."

"Well, this is different. This time I'm askin'."

She fumbled with a button and slowly let it come undone. Then she started on another one. "You know they ain't no way we kin do anything. You'd just grab me."

"I can look, can't I? did you know that, depending on the woman, it's more exciting to see a lady with just her hose and garters on and maybe her step-ins. Maybe even her camisole. That is, if they are right nice stuff like yours."

She looked interested, and he noticed her breathing had quickened slightly. "Is that right? I never heared that before."

"Aw, yeah. Kind of like the wrapping on a present. All that pretty paper and ribbons."

"You mean it's more excitin' than just, you know, her nakid?"

"Well, you get down to that at the end. But starting out, it's exciting to see a woman like that. Kind of like peeking around the door and into her bedroom when she don't know you're there."

She undid another button, and now her bodice was open down to the top of her apron. "Is that a fact?"

"Know what I'd like?" he said, watching her.

"What?"

"I'd like to see you just in your apron. Nothing on top, and nothing underneath. Just them silk stockings and your apron. Then you could stand there and kind of slowly lift that apron up. Just take it up a little bit at a time. Boy, that would drive me crazy." He took a drink out of his glass, watching her over the rim. He could see her bosom rising and falling and a little color rising in her face. She picked up the fan out of her lap and waved it back and forth in front of her face, but he knew it wasn't the outside heat that was bothering her.

"Yeah," he said softly, "that would be something to see. You just in that apron with them stockings on, maybe red garters and—"

"They pink," she said breathlessly. "Pink an' white."

"What?"

"My garters. They is pink and white."

"Mmmmm," he said. "That's even better." He licked his lips. "Boy, that would be a sight."

She fanned harder, and he could see her squirming in her chair. She said faintly, "This ain't right. We oughtn't to be talkin' like this."

He said soothingly, "Lily Gail, it's my time. Oughtn't I to get to use it however I want?" His intentions were nothing less than to try and heat her up from across the distance separating them so she would jump out of her chair and rush to his arms, apron pocket and keys and all. He knew it was a long shot, but he also knew that Lily Gail was as strongly sexed as any woman he'd ever met. And he knew, from little signs and things she'd said, that it wouldn't take much more to push her over the line to where she'd be willing to help him.

But she suddenly jumped up. She said, her breath coming in gasps, "This ain't good fer you, Custis. And you with such a little time left. I won't do this to you."

And with that she turned and almost ran out of the barn.

He watched her go and then slumped back in his chair. He'd overplayed his hand. He shouldn't have said that about his "time" and using it however he wanted. He should have just kept on talking about lingerie; that had been working. He sighed and took a long drink of the lemonade and whiskey. If it hadn't been for wasting the whiskey he'd have poured the mess out of his glass. He'd only taken it in hopes of pleasing Lily Gail.

Aloud he said, "Boy, Longarm, you are really gettin' to be some kind of a whore. Or an apple polisher, or something. You are about as phony as a tomcat in a cattle herd."

He sat there, and a man nammed Tom Mullins came to his mind, a deputy marshal that Longarm had worked with a few times in Colorado and the New Mexico Territory. He recalled several years back when Mullins had been pursuing some bandits through some mountains in northern New Mexico and a rock slide had come down and buried him. As luck would have it, he'd been able to dive into a little indentation in the side of the mountain before the rock slide had come over. It had left him in a little space about the size of Billy Vail's desk. He'd finally been dug out by a party that had been coming along behind him, but it had taken many hours before he was able to see the sky. Longarm had asked him what he'd done all that time and Mullins had said, "I done it simple. I just kept on breathing. I knew as long as I kept on breathing I'd be all right."

Which was true in his case. All he had to do was concentrate on continued breathing. The Gallaghers might want to interrupt that, but until they did he would be all right.

Lily Gail came back. She looked composed and a little stern. She sat down and said, "Now, Custis, we can't have any more of that." She fingered the buttons she'd redone. "It ain't good fer you. I know a man has got wants and needs and desires and they got to be met from time to time. But they ain't no way we can tend to them. That ought to be plain enough. So you've just got to quit thinkin' them thoughts."

He said, "Well, Lily Gail, I don't see how I can keep from it. Not with you sittin' there lookin' like the frosting on a cake."

She looked uncertain. "Maybe I ought to go."

"No, no, no," he said. "It's too lonesome out here. Especially for a man about to . . ." He let the thought lapse, leaving it to her imagination.

"I done said I was sorry fer what I done to you last night. Now I'm tryin' to make up fer it, even if what I done was caused by some mighty bad proddin' from you. But now I'm tryin' to be good."

He looked down at the barn floor as if he were being shy. "They ought to be something we can do, Lily Gail."

"Well, if you can think of anything we can do ten feet apart, I'll be glad to go along with it. But I shore ain't never heered of nothin'."

"I just can't get the picture of you in that apron out of my mind. I've done grabbed you once and turned you loose. Ain't that proof enough?"

102

She thought about it for a moment and then slowly shook her head. "I jest can't be shore. I mean, ain't nothin' I'd like more than to git you up next to me one more time, but I got a lot to lose here."

"You got a lot more to lose if you don't turn me loose, Lily Gail. I'm not kidding abou. that. You help the Gallaghers to kill me and Eugene will have got out of prison and grown a long gray beard before you ever see daylight again."

But she was serene. "Gallaghers won't let nothin' happen to me. And with that big chunk 'o cash I'll git, why, ain't no tellin' where I'll go."

He studied her. There was something very cowlike about Lily Gail, very placid. She had an idea firmly implanted in her mind, and neither he nor anyone else was going to shake her out of it.

"Lily Gail, how old are you?"

She put her hand to her mouth and giggled. "Oh, now! An' I thought you was such a gentleman. My, my, you know it ain't perlite to ast a lady her age."

"I know you're young, how young doesn't matter. But I know you are too young to waste the rest of your life over one foolish mistake."

She sighed. "Thar you go again. Custis, I can see yore point of view on this matter. I can indeed. Was I in the same fix, I might try some of them same arguments you been usin' on me. But I kin see through them. See, my conscience is clear. When Rufus er Emmet er whoever comes fer you gets here, I'm jest gonna turn my head whilst they pack you off. The last I'll see of you you'll be alive and well an' jest as hansom as ever. An' if they are a-gonna do it here, why, I'll just go on into town an' stay thar a few days. Custis, I won't never know what become of you. Fact of the business, I'm thinkin' 'bout

103

hitchin' up that buggy tomorrow mornin' and lightin' out *afore* they git here."

He shook his head. "I can't believe you can mean that about having a clear conscience. You know well and good what they plan for me. And you could turn me loose now. You could go with me. I'd see right by you. I'd see that you got money and a place to live. Hell, if you were in any way responsible for the capture of the Gallaghers, you'd get hell's own kind of money in the reward."

But she just looked complacent. "Custis, I cain't do that. I've knowed the Gallaghers ever since I was a little girl."

"Is that how you got mixed up with them?"

She shrugged. "Around this part of the territory, you is either with the Gallaghers er you are agin 'em. Them that is agin 'em don't last very long. They got enough kin to fight Mexico, I would reckon."

He could see that he was arguing against a lifetime of experience and prejudice. "Did you get close, I mean on the inside like you are now, when you married Bob Drago?"

"Oh, Bob wasn't my first husband. I was actually married to a Gallagher, though he was just a great-nephew to ol' Devil Jacob Gallagher. I think he was a second cousin to Vern or Clem, the main ones with Rufus. I mean since they daddy died."

"They are all going to die, Lily Gail. And you with them if you are not careful. I'm not just trying to save my hide when I tell you how serious it is to kill a federal officer. I'm thinking about you."

"Oh, I wouldn't doubt you are. But like I say, when they ast me questions about you, I'll be able to say last time I saw you you was gettin' plenty to eat an' was

104

smokin' a cigar an' drankin' whiskey."

He stared at her. He could see he had very little chance of reaching her with logic. Behind the ridge-pole was the heavy coffee mug. He considered taking a shot at her head with it. She was only about twelve feet away, and if he hit her solid, it would certainly knock her out, maybe kill her. She'd be out of his reach, but he might be able to stretch enough to get to the hay rake and drag her apron over. But as he weighed the chances, he decided to save it for one last desperate measure. She'd left the hay rake in what appeared to be a position too far away for his reach.

"Whatever happened to your first husband, Lily Gail?"

"Oh, Rufus kilt him."

It startled him, the offhanded way she said it. "Just like that?"

"Well, naw, he had his reasons. Johnny had gotten kind of light-fingered when he was handlin' some of the holdup money that belonged to them all. So they laid a trap fer him an' he got caught. So Rufus jest up and blowed him in two with a shotgun."

"He shot your husband and you are still willing to do his work for him?"

"Rufus was mighty nice about it. He told me ahead of time what was goin' on and what he would have to do."

"And you didn't warn your husband?"

She shook her head. "Why, no. He had it comin' if he was stealin' from his own kin. Besides, he was another one of them handy sonofabitches like Bob Drago, especially when he had strong drink in him, which was all the time. I never have figgered why some men feel they got to beat up on a woman jest to show how tough they

105

is. Maybe it's a good time for 'em. Besides, I was just turnin' nineteen at the time and I didn't know nothin'."

"Well, you've seen me drink. I never laid a hand on you. And I wouldn't."

She smiled coyly. "Oh, I don't know. Thar fer a little while in bed I thought you had five or six hands."

"You know what I mean."

"Course I do, Custis. And I want you to know if I could he'p you I would. I hate to think of not, you know, havin' any more fun with you." She leaned forward a little and lowered her voice as if they might be overheard. "I ain't ever gonna forget how you picked me up and carried me round the room on yore . . . you know. Like it was that, that ramrod thang of yours was holdin' me up. I am shore gonna miss yore ways."

"We could have some more."

"How?"

He thought. "What if I was to hold real still and you tied my hands behind my back. You'd have to do most of the work, but you wouldn't have to worry about me grabbing you."

She gave him a doubtful look. "Shore," she said. "You are a-gonna stand there right still while I tie yore hands. Anybody got tied up would be me."

"You get a long piece of rope and I'll knot one end around my wrist and then make a running hitch on the other, behind my back, and then you just jerk on the end of the long rope and *wham*, I'm hogtied. After that you can figure out what you want to do." He smiled. "I guess you might could say you'd have the run of the place."

She dabbed her tongue around her lips, thinking. "Well, maybe. Though I'd have to be good and shore you was tied tight."

"I would be," he said. In his eagerness he took a hard pull off the lemonade glass and almost gagged. He swore to himself that he would rather be in a six-against-one gunfight than try to trick this stupid girl. She was so damn dumb that things that ought to work on her went right over her head. Her only vulnerability was right between her legs and he had to keep working that angle. He felt as if he was in the fight of his life.

She said, "Let's just not talk about it right now. It gets me all hot and bothered, and lordy, it is hot enough already." She picked up the fan and began to stir air around her face. Then she leaned forward so that her bodice gaped open and fanned down the front of her dress.

One thing he would give her, he thought. She wasn't much for brains, but she had about as pretty a set of breasts as he'd ever chanced across.

Chapter 6

"Lily Gail, what's the situation on the whiskey in the house? Is this the last bottle?" He held it up. It was only half full.

"Lord, no," she said. "Rufus left plenty whiskey, and so did Emmett. And they is plenty of cigars." She looked uncomfortable. "Though I ain't sure you'll have time to go through all them."

"What makes you think that the Gallaghers will kill me? You may not know it, but they'll damn sure know what comes of killing a federal marshal."

The lemonade was gone and she sat with an empty glass in her hand. She'd undone her top buttons again, but he hadn't commented on it. She said matter-of-factly, " 'Cause they hate yore guts. They say you are harder to shake than a summer cold an' they is tired of havin' you on their tracks."

He took a drink of straight whiskey and thought of that for a moment. He said, "They know that ain't got nothing to do with it. *Every* marshal is a burr under their saddle blanket." He nodded his head sideways at the haystack. "Lily Gail, do you know what is under that hay?"

"Course. Dynamite and such. Bullets and I don't know what all. Why?"

He looked at her in amazement. "Doesn't that make you nervous having that around?"

She said primly, "Rufus and them knows what they is doin'. They said to jest stay away from it an' it wasn't no more dangerous than a milk cow."

"Unless this barn was to catch on fire."

She shrugged. "Oh, that. Ain't no reason fer that to happen. This ain't thunderstorm season. It ain't gonna lightnin'."

"What about me smoking in here?"

She laughed. "Well! If you know what's in yonder under that hay, I reckon you'd be the one would be mighty careful."

"You got any idea what they got that stored here for?"

"Oh, yeah. They gonna blow up the bank in Lawton and rob it."

He stared at her, surprised in spite of himself. "Do what?"

"They's a whole bunch of money comin' down fer them Indian Affairs folks. You know, them ones as runs the reservations fer all them heathens. Gonna be pretty quick. So Rufus plans to blow out the wall of the bank so's they can git in an' out right quick."

"When did they plan this?"

"Oh, they been figgerin' on it right along. See, Rufus, an' them got an in at the reservations, an' they git word when big loads of money is comin' in. But they know that thar Lawton bank is a tough nut to crack. Them was Rufus's very own words so he just said, 'By golly, I'll jest blow her to hell 'n back.' That's what he said when be brung the dynamite they robbed off some army place. Got a bunch of bullets too."

Longarm looked at her steadily. "How'd you like to be walking by that bank when they set it off?"

She gave him a strange look. "Why, I wouldn't care fer it at all. But then I ain't gonna be doin' no such damn fool thing, am I?"

"No, but some innocent people will be."

"Well, that's they lookout. Ain't no affair of mine." She got up. "I reckon I better get on in the house an' git to cookin'. That is, if we are to have some supper. How you feel about beef hash?"

"I like it," he said. But his mind was still on the dynamite and the offhanded way she'd told him how it was going to be used. He wondered if they'd maybe include him in the blast when they blew up the bank. Be a hell of a way to get rid of a federal marshal, scatter him over several counties. He wondered just when the reservation money was due in at the Lawton bank. Usually money intended for the Indian Affairs department, for use on the reservations, which the Oklahoma Territory was full of, came in gold and coins since the Indians didn't much trust white man's paper.

She said, "Them potatoes I got are gettin' kind of moldy, so I reckon I'll just take the balance of that roast beef and chop it up and hash it. That sound good to you?"

"Oh, yes," he said, still looking over at the hay.

"I got some canned tomaters also. You want some of them?"

"Just mix it all together. I'll eat it."

"They's some beer. You want a couple bottles of that to drank?"

He looked up at her, "Of course."

"Well, I'll go fix it and then I'll bring it out here an' we'll eat together. You want to do that?"

"Oh, yeah. Make it taste better."

At the door of the barn she stopped and turned around. "You know what you was sayin'? 'Bout how we might figger somethin' out?"

"Yeah?"

"I been thinkin' on it. Might just be a way. Somethin' Rufus left. Said I might have some use fer it in case I got you to come to my honey."

"What?"

She gave him a sly smile. "What you care long as you git what you want?"

"You ain't gonna tell me?"

"I got to think on it an' see if it'll work. I don't know if I can find the blamed things. You don't mind eatin' early, do you? We might need to git supper out the way."

"I'm hungry now."

He was watching her, wondering what she was up to. He said, "don't forget to bring me some more whiskey and cigars and matches. Especially matches. Some of mine got wet when I took my bath."

She said, "I noticed you looked all nice an' clean. I got to hand it to you, Custis, ain't many a man would take that kind 'o care of hisself with what you got starin' you in the face."

"You not going to tell me what you got in mind?"

"If it'll do, let's us make it a surprise. Like Christmas or yore birthday."

He shrugged and left it at that.

The supper was good. He ate off the tray, balanced on his knees, while Lily Gail sat ten feet away and ate off the little table. She drank lemonade and he drank the two bottles of beer she'd brought him. They kept the conversation light, mostly talking about the towns they'd visited, trying to figure if they knew anyone in common outside of the Gallaghers and Kyle Greenwood. Lily Gail had been in Texas, Oklahoma, Arkansas, and Louisiana, once nearly to New Orleans. Houston was the biggest town she'd ever been in, and that was when she was a girl of eighteen. The highlight of that trip had been a man coming up and offering her a job in his saloon. "Why, it was the craziest thing," she said. "I ast him what I was supposed to do an' he said nothin'. Jest set around and get men to buy a lot of drinks an' make shore they had a good time. Ain't that the craziest thang you ever heard of?"

"It leads to other kinds of work."

"What kind of work?"

He winked at her. "You said you didn't want me getting worked up for no cause."

She said mysteriously, "We might just have us a cause. I just think it might work. That is if you are a-willin'."

He stopped his fork halfway to his mouth. "If you're talking about what I think you're talking about, I am way long gone more than willing. Are you talking about what we were talking about earlier when you made me quit talking about it?"

"Now you jest never mind. Put your attention to that apple cobbler I made. I know it's canned apples, but that's all I had an' that old stove don't cook worth a durn. Naturally I din't have no cream to put over it, but you eat it up or you'll hurt my feelin's." She gave him a sly smile. "An' I don't reckon you want to hurt my feelin's."

"No indeed," he said.

113

It was about five-thirty in the afternoon when he shoved his dishes over to her on the tray, using the hay rake. It took her two trips to take everything back in the house. Then she came back and said, "Now you jest set there and have your smoke and drank yore whiskey. I'm gonna see if I cain't get this here thought of mine to work. I'll be back right after it gets dark."

He sat there, wishing the sun to go down faster, his mind playing with all sorts of thoughts and plans and possibilities. He hadn't the slightest idea what she was alluding to, except it had to do with the talk they'd had that afternoon about her in an apron and tying his hands behind his back. He did not dare let himself hope that she would be fool enough to believe he'd actually tie himself in such a manner that he couldn't get loose and get hold of her and her apron and the keys. But yet, he couldn't think what else she could be talking about. Surely she wasn't just going to come to him willingly. The joke would be on him if she came into the barn naked and was ready to give herself to him. How would he then ask her where her apron was? That would be the final irony. He'd spent the better part of a day making the fool girl believe he was willing to die happy if he could just have one more piece of her—apron included, of course. And now, if all that sappy talk just resulted in her and no keys . . . Well, what a dying laugh that would be on him.

So he just sat and smoked and drank whiskey and watched the sun finally begin to flatten itself against the far horizon outside the barn door. It was, he reckoned, the longest dusk he'd ever gone through.

She showed up about an hour after dark. She must have let herself out of the kitchen door quietly because he didn't hear it slam. The first indication he had of her

114

coming was when he saw the ghostly light from a lantern and then saw it get brighter and brighter as she neared the barn door.

She came to the door, stopped for just a second, and then took five or six steps in his direction. She held up the lantern to just above her shoulder. He could see she was wearing only her apron and the pink silk stockings with white garters. She said huskily, "This what you had on yore mind?"

He could feel his heart beating like a triphammer. He breathed, "Oh, my, yes. Come a little closer, honey, so I can see you better."

She took several more steps toward him. In the lantern's glow, against the pitch black of the barn door, she looked like an alabaster statue with her breasts standing erect and her pink nipples sticking out like not-quite-ripe strawberries. She had the lantern in her right hand and there was something hanging from her left hand, but he couldn't quite make it out.

"You ready for me to raise my apron a lettle?"

"Oh, yeah." He dropped off the chair and knee-walked a yard or so toward her.

She dropped whatever was in her left hand. It made a slight clanking noise as it fell on the hay-covered floor. Then, with tantalizing slowness she took the middle of her apron, clutching it in her hand, and began to slowly lift it. In spite of his rapt attention on the slowly rising hem of the apron, he distinctly heard the slight jangle of the keys as they turned over in her apron pocket.

But his real attention was on that rising apron. It came up above her knees and then halfway up her thighs to where the pink and white garters were, and then the stockings ended and her milk-white thighs began, starting to narrow as they funneled toward the prize.

And then it was coming in sight, the little patch of V-shaped curly light brown hair, standing out in stark relief against the complete nakedness of her body.

"Oooh, my!" he said huskily. He began unbuttoning his jeans. "Honey, you got to come here. I can't take this."

She lowered the lantern so she could use both hands to untie her apron. She let it fall to her feet and then stood there, the light shining up at her, making her breasts stand out, with her little rounded belly and the little mound where the curly hair grew. It had surprised him, her dropping her apron like that. It made a distinct sound as it hit the floor of the barn. Hell, he thought, where is the hay rake? That was the only way he'd be able to snag that apron and pull it over once he got hold of her. But, too late, he saw that it was to his right and just a few feet out of his reach, even if he stretched out to his full length. She'd taken it from him after he'd pushed his dishes and tray to her, and had just dropped it.

But he could figure that out later. What he had to do now was to get his hands on her. On his knees, with his jeans down to the floor, he held out his hands. "Come on, honey. I can't stand much more."

She pointed. "Oh, my, look at you. Look at that big ol' thang. You gonna put that in little me?"

"All the way up to your throat," he said huskily. "Come on."

But instead of moving, she bent down and picked up the metallic thing he'd heard hit the floor. Now he could see that it looked like some kind of chain.

"What in hell is that?"

"I'm gonna pitch it over to you. It's a kind of wrist thang to chain yore hands behind yore back."

He stared. "What?"

116

"Look out. I'm fixin' to pitch it."

And the next instant the apparatus came flying through the air and landed at his knees right in front of him. He picked it up curiously. It was like the handcuffs he used, except there was about two and half feet of chain between the wrist manacles that joined together with teeth that snapped into place. He said, "Lily Gail, you don't want me to put this on, do you?"

"You got to," she said earnestly. "It's the onliest way I can chance it. You got to cuff yore hands behind yore back."

"But how are we going to do anything that way?"

She stepped a little closer and held the lantern higher. "Don't you worry. I'll do all the work, honey. You won't lose nothin'. I promise you."

He said doubtfully, "You have got the key to these, haven't you? And where did you get such things?"

"Oh, it was some of the stuff that Rufus took offen that army depot. They was stuff I thank he said they used on the Injuns. They was some of the same thangs for the legs, but I didn't figure you needed no more than what you already got on yore laig."

He turned the wrist manacles one way and then another, looking for a flaw. But there didn't appear to be any. Once you shoved the ratchet home in the socket hole you were manacled. He said, "I'm just disappointed you don't trust me more."

"Aw, honey," she said. "Don't take on like that. It's the onliest way. And look at you, you're lettin' yore thang go down."

He looked back at her, inspiring himself with the sight of her body. "But you do have the keys for this? I don't want to get bound up like this and not be able to even feed myself."

117

She said, "Oh, yes, I got the keys. I even tried them." She motioned back behind her. "They in the pocket of my apron. You kin take 'em off after we are done." She looked at him appealingly. "I thought you'd just love my little surprise."

"Oh, I do, I do," he said. But his mind was calculating if it would interfere with what he had in mind. It would make it harder, that was for sure, but it could still be done. And he had to take the chance because he might not get another one. He said, tapping one of the wrist manacles, "These are going to be kind of hard to lay on."

"Oh, no. They's enough play that you kin get yore hands out to yore sides. In fact, if I get around to your back you got plenty room to play with me." He could see her blush faintly in the lantern light.

He looked up at her and smiled. "You already tried them?"

"Oh, yes."

"Why don't we put them on you, then?"

She giggled. "Hurry up, honey. I'm just all afahr inside. My coals is about to flame up."

He gingerly put one of the hinged cuffs around his wrist and pushed the ratched tongue into the hole. It went *clitch-clitch-clitch*. He had thought that he could put them on loose enough that he could slip his hands out, but the cuffs were made for hands much smaller than his, and even the first notch of the teeth fitted snugly enough that he knew he could never get his hand out.

She said, "Now turn around and let me watch you put on the other'n."

"You just don't trust me at all."

"Oh, honey, it ain't that. Rufus would jest kill me if I wuz to let you git away. The day Emmett rode out of here it was too late."

That, he thought to himself, is what you think.

But with his back to her so she could watch him, he ratched the other manacle onto his right wrist. He tugged, pulling at them, trying to pull them apart. "You satisfied? You got me trussed up like a pig for market. What do we do now?"

With a little shortness of breath she said, "You look at me fer a minute and then you lie down on yore back."

She did as she had the night she'd tormented him. She set the lantern down on the floor and then slowly ran her hands up and down her body, moving them slowly over her breasts and then stroking her abdomen down toward the little forested mound at the V of her legs. He watched, his breath coming hard in spite of what he knew he was going to do. She was letting her fingers stroke in between her legs, teasing the silken hair. He could hear her breathing across the ten feet that separated them. He lay back, moving carefully to get his hands to the side so the manacles wouldn't dig into his flesh. They just barely cleared his thighs. They might have been plenty big enough for Lily Gail, but they were snug on him. He could also feel the chain under him, but by shifting around he got it into a place that wasn't too uncomfortable.

Now Lily Gail had approached until she was standing just at his feet. She'd brought the lantern, setting it well to the side so they couldn't upset it, but it still gave enough light so that he could see her fingers working her lips apart and showing him the warm pinkness inside. By then she was breathing heavily and her breasts were heaving.

She suddenly bent down, going down on all fours, coming up to him and kissing him on the mouth and then on the neck and the ears. Then she moved up and slowly put one nipple after another in his mouth. He was panting so hard he was almost gasping for breath.

Slowly she began to kiss her way down his body, sliding her tongue down his flat abdomen. Suddenly he was in her mouth and he arched his back and groaned, almost crying out. He said frantically, "Careful, careful!"

She straightened up. "I'm going to get it now," she said. With her hand she guided him deep inside her. He almost cried out with the sensation of the wet warmth. Then she began to slowly and rhythmically rise up and down on him as she rotated from side to side.

"Oh!" she said. "Oh! That's jest right!"

She was gyrating faster now, her upper body flinging itself back and forth so that her hair flew and her breasts bobbed up and down. "I can't stand it!" She made a little half scream that he knew meant she was getting very close.

He was in the devil of a predicament. He knew what he had to do and that it had to be done with perfect timing and precision. And that called for a cool head. But it was very difficult to keep a cool head with all the heat surging around and through him. And meanwhile he had to keep himself interested in her in order to give her something stiff to work with. It was a hell of a dilemma, but one that might suddenly solve itself. He could feel the thrust rising up from his own loins.

Then she exploded and solved his problems for him. She let out a loud scream and threw her head back, arching her back as she did. In that instant he jerked up his legs, locked them around her neck and throat, and plucked her over backward. She was torn loose from him, her legs going flying in his face as the downward move of his legs brought him to a sitting position. For a second the sudden development left her stunned. But then she began to screech and scream and flail with her arms and legs. There was nothing he could do to keep her from kicking and hitting him, not with his hands behind his back, so all he could do was squeeze with his powerful legs. He yelled, as loud as he could because he knew that his legs were partly covering her ears and because she was yelling so loud herself, "Lily Gail! Lily Gail! Lily Gail, goddammit, Listen to me!"

But she continued to flail her arms and kick her legs and twist her body around. One of her kicks caught Longarm in the nose. It hurt, and after a second he could feel the blood dripping down on his lip. It made him angry, and he added more pressure to the head-lock he had on Lily Gail. He yelled, "Goddammit, Lily Gail, I'll break your damn head wide open you don't be still!"

He could hear some muffled words coming from the tangle of hair between his knees. The way he had her, her face was sideways and slightly downward. He said, "Shut up and listen!"

Either she tired out, or he was choking her to where she couldn't breathe, or she was finally beginning to understand she was struggling in vain, because her flailing and kicking finally subsided until she was lying still. He let up on the pressure just a little, and she instantly began to thrash around again. He clamped back down, harder this time. "Goddammit, Lily Gail, you better understand that you are caught and quit hurting yourself!"

Now she made some sort of muffled sounds and lay still. He never felt more frustrated in his life with his hands manacled behind him. All he had was that slim hold on her with his legs. It was difficult to tell how tight to hold her. Too tight and he might hurt her, might even strangle her or break her neck. Not tight enough and she could slip her head out and be gone in a flash.

And then she slid off on his left side and kicked back with one of her feet. It landed exactly in the palm of his left hand. Instinctively he grabbed her around the ankle, his big hand going completely around it with room to spare. She made a little groan and tried to jerk it loose, but she might as well have tried to pull it out of well-set concrete.

He said, "If I loosen up on your head will you listen? I got you by the foot so you ain't going nowhere."

She made some muffled sounds, which he figured out to mean, "You dirty lyin' sonofabitch!"

He said, "I don't blame you for your feelings, Lily Gail. But I am fighting for my life here. Now, I don't want to hurt you, but I will if you don't do exactly like I say, you understand?"

She turned her head a little—he'd relaxed his grip enough for that—and said, "Go to hell, you bastard. I's tryin' to be nice to you an'—"

He didn't let her finish, just clamped down with his muscular, powerful legs until he could feel her writhing in pain. When he felt her going limp he eased the pressure. "Lily Gail, you better get it straight in your mind what is gonna happen here. You are going to help me get your apron over here that has got the keys in it or you ain't going to get out of here. You understand me?"

She didn't move and she didn't say anything for a moment. He started to increase the pressure again, but she began beating him on the leg and said, "Wait, wait! Wait a minute, can'tcha?"

He eased up. "Well? Do you understand?"

"You done played a dirty trick on me, Custis Long. I hate you again."

"Woman, are you crazy? Did you think I was just going to sit here quietly and be murdered by the Gallaghers? I didn't play a *dirty* trick on you. I played a trick on you. Was my trick dirtier than the one you pulled on me with that whiskey and laudanum? Huh? Huh? Answer that one."

She was silent. Then, after a few seconds, he thought he could hear her sniffling quietly. He said, "Oh, hell, you ain't cryin', are you? Now don't start that nonsense on me, Lily Gail. I ain't got time for it."

She muffled out, "Wa'l, I never played no trick on you when we was doin' it!"

In other circumstances he would have laughed. But not now. In the first place he felt the press of time. The Gallaghers or Emmett could ride up anytime. And he was helpless. He sat there, his hands behind his back, his legs around her neck, her ankle in his hand, and assessed the situation. He could see the end of the rake, and he knew that she wouldn't be able to reach it the way he was holding her. He would have to get her around the waist, and that was going to be a tricky move, somehow slipping her forward through his legs without her getting away.

He said, "I want you to lift yourself up."

"What?"

"I want you to get up on your hands and knees."

"You jest go to hell, mister. You ain't havin' no more of me."

He said, his voice low and deadly, "Lily Gail, that is going to be the last time I give you an order and you don't do it. Next time I'll crush your head. You understand me?"

123

"You wouldn't kill no lady."

"You want to bet your life on that?" He said it with quiet deadliness.

She was quiet while she thought if he meant it or not. She'd heard a great many stories about this man they called Longarm. They had said he was tough, he was fair, he was tireless, he was fearless, he was deadly, he was a lot of things. But one thing she'd never heard was that he was a liar. In fact she had heard Rufus say, "One the reasons we got to git this sumbitch is he swore to run us to ground. We got to do to him 'fore he does to us."

He said, "I'm gonna give you a very few more seconds to get up on your hands and knees."

She said querulously, "How kin I with them damn heavy ol' laigs of your'n a-layin' on me?"

He lifted his top leg slightly, just enough for her to raise up slightly, but not enough for her to find room to bolt. As she raised up a little more he raised his top leg, all the while keeping his ankles locked and ready to clamp back down if she made the slightest false move.

Little by little she worked her way up until she was on her hands and knees on the barn floor and he had his lower legs locked around her head and neck at the ankles. He wanted to get her around the waist. But to do that he couldn't simply slide his legs up her body because her arms were in the way. He was going to have to unlock his ankles, drag his legs back, and then grab her around the waist before she could react. He still had hold of one of her ankles with his left hand, but if she were to roll or twist her body he wouldn't be able to hold her because of the immobility of his hand, caught as it was by the manacle.

At one point he had mistakenly thought he could get her up close to him and then slide his hands under his own body and under hers and have his chained hands in front of him. That would have been ideal, and he probably wouldn't even have needed her to get the hay rake to pull in her apron. He'd have been able to do it himself.

But then had come the realization that he couldn't pass the manacle chain under his feet because of the logging chain that was around his ankle. He was indeed trussed up like a Christmas pig.

He had tried every way he could think of to somehow work his arms around to where the chain would pass over the top of his head, but his shoulder joints just weren't built that way.

So it came down to the fact that he was going to have to use Lily Gail as an extension of himself to reach the hay rake. Once the hay rake was in his hands, the apron was close enough that he could get it himself. And once he had the keys Lily Gail could jump and run as far as she wanted, just so long as she didn't run for a gun. He didn't think she would stray too far the way she was dressed.

He looked down at her. Her head was obscured by his legs and she was supporting a good bit of him the way they were placed. She was sort of quartering off his left side at a small angle. He thought he could hear her snuffling again. He said, "Now what's the matter? I know I'm not squeezing hard enough to hurt you."

She said, between little sobs, "I—I guess you, you know that you have durn near 'bout ruint my stockin's. An' them the onliest pair o' silk ones I got." His jeans were down around his ankles, mostly on the other side of her head, but one of the legs had apparently, somehow, gotten wound around her neck, and she took a second to clear it before she said tearfully, "That was jest right down mean. Ruinin' my stockin's in all this dirt 'n mud."

At that instant he jerked his legs out of his jeans, nipped the top one over her head, knocked her arms out from under her with his left—the one encumbered by the chain, got them both back to her waist, and clamped on to her again just above her hips. With a bend of his knees he pulled her up into his naked crotch, in between his strong thighs. The move had dropped her on her face, but he'd caught her around the middle before she could go all the way down.

She cussed furiously for a second. "You are really a mean bastard. I cain't believe I was gonna be in love with you."

"Me either," he said. "Bad things seem to happen to them you love. Your two husbands, for instance." He put his hands flat on the ground and pivoted on his buttocks, carrying her along. "You see just yonder? A few feet up toward the front of the barn. That's the hay rake. I'm gonna scoot you up there and you are going to get hold of the end and hand it to me."

She had slumped down on the ground. "No, I ain't."

He sighed. "Lily Gail, you ought to be able to figure out that I am in a kind of desperate position here and I ain't got a whole hell of a lot of time. I don't want to hurt you to make you do this, but I will if I have to."

"You done a downright dirty thang to me. What you done when we was doin' it an' I was just about to feel it. Jerkin' me back by the head like that. Near to broke my neck an' then you near smothered the breath outten me. And ain't none of that to mention you ruinin' my onliest pair of silk stockin's. I ain't gonna help you a lick."

Longarm sighed. To the best of his knowledge he had never deliberately hurt a woman physically. He might have hurt a few emotionally, but that wasn't anything he could do anything about. But physically, no. Oh, he'd had a few wildcats come at him with fingernails and knives and various other implements, and he'd been forced to subdue them. But he was certain he'd never before set out to deliberately cause a woman physical pain to get her to do something. Still, he didn't know what else to do. He'd appealed to Lily Gail's good sense, only to find she didn't have any. He'd swallowed his pride and appealed to her pity, and that hadn't done any good. He'd tried logic on her, with no results. He'd wooed her with honeyed words that had nearly made him sick to his stomach. And now he was at a place where he had to make her help him and he didn't seem to have any choice. He said, "Lily Gail, you ain't giving me no selection. It ain't my style to hurt a woman, but I've got to have your help and if hurting you is the only way I can get it, then I reckon that's the way it'll have to be. But I want you to think about it before I commence. All I got is this grip on you with my legs and all I can do is squeeze. But hell, Lily Gail, you're just a little bit of a woman. I bet you don't weigh much more than a hundred pounds. And these old legs of mine are mighty strong. I've used these legs to stay on broncs didn't want me on their backs, so you can get some kind of idea of the power I'm liable to use on you." He stopped and shook his shoulders. "Damn! I'm getting a cramp in my back. Son of a bitch! Damn that hurts!"

After a moment it passed. He said, "The point I'm trying to make is that I ain't sure how hard a man like me has to squeeze a little woman like you to hurt her real bad. I mean, like cause you some serious damage.

Break your back or something. Hell, Lily Gail, why don't you just make this easy on both of us and say you'll help me?"

"I done said I ain't an' I ain't. Rufus would skin me 'live."

"Rufus!" His temper got out of hand. "Rufus! You silly little bitch, they's a damn good chance he'll be skinning a corpse by the time I get through with you."

"You'll be one of them too. Them corpses. I don' he'p you, you gonna be settin' right here with me between yore laigs when he gits here."

"Well, at least I'm gonna put you in a position where you can help if you change your mind."

With an effort, using his hands to push with and jerking her sideways with his legs, he propelled them as far as the chain would let him. The end of the rake was tantalizingly close. If he'd had a three-foot gaff with a hook on it, he could have dragged it in. All Lily Gail would have to do was stretch out and reach out with her arm and it would come to hand.

He said, "Lily Gail, raise up your head. Raise up your head and look just a few feet toward the barn door."

She did not raise her head, but she shook it back and forth defiantly. "No, I tell you. I ain't gonna he'p you. You better git that idee through yore thick head."

He said gently, "Lily Gail, you are going to do this. If it comes to it, I'll strike a match and light a cigar and burn the soles of your feet. Why do you want to suffer this pain when you don't have to?"

"Yore hands is behind yore back. You can't strike no matches."

"I have got a good deal more play with my hands than you think." For illustration he moved his left hand up to her pubic hair and gave it a hard yank.

"Owww!" she said. "You low-down, goddamn son-ofabitch!"

"See, you ain't as brave as you thought you were. Now raise your head and hand me that rake. The matches and my cigars are right at hand. But I'm gonna squeeze you first."

"You go to Hell."

He set his jaw and began squeezing with his thighs. Instantly she went rigid. As he slowly increased the pressure she began to moan and then to groan loudly. He had some protection for his vitals in the way he had her body jammed up in his crotch. But just to be sure he was protected, he had worked both hands around until the chain allowed him enough slack to cover his privates with his left hand.

As he squeezed harder she began to gasp and then make little screaming noises. She began to claw and hit at him. He could see the bloody scratches she was making on his legs, but he didn't care about that. As long as his vital parts were protected, there wasn't anything she could do that would hurt him.

He squeezed harder, and for a second she let out a loud, piercing scream, but then it gurgled off to nothing as she began to have the breath squeezed out of her.

But it was almost as hard on him. Once he felt like something had broken, and for an instant, he started to slacken off, but then one of her garters flew off, and he realized it was just the elastic that had broken with her wild flailing around.

He kept up the pressure relentlessly. "Lily Gail, when you are ready to help, just nod your head and I'll stop. You hear me?"

His face was sweating, his whole body was sweating. He was almost convinced that it was hurting her worse than him. And the hell of it was that he didn't know how far to go. How much pressure did it take to snap her backbone? How much to turn her innards into mashed potatoes? He was already squeezing so hard that he had his jaw clenched.

Her breath now was coming in shallow gasps. He was amazed she could breathe at all. No longer was she flailing or scratching at him. Her arms and legs lay limp. He suddenly released the pressure and let his legs relax. She responded with a great, agonizing gasp of air. Then she slowly lifted her head and began to pant. In the lantern's glow he could see her hair, matted and wet with sweat. Her whole body, where it wasn't soiled with the barn floor dirt, glistened with sweat. She lay between his thighs, panting, gasping. She said, mumbling, "Oh, you sorry bastard."

"You ready to help?"

"Go to Hell."

He instantly clamped down on her middle, forcing a scream out of her that had started out as a gasp. "Help me, Lily Gail. Help me. You want to die?"

Through gritted teeth she said, "You ain't gonna kill me. No good to you if you kill me."

She kept coming back to that point and there was no way around it for him. She was right. And he might accidentally kill her.

But he kept up the relentless pressure, trying to make her break, trying to force the pain to overcome her spirit.

He said, "You that stubborn? Or are you that afraid of Rufus? Which is it? Or do you just hate me so much?"

She didn't reply, just lay there panting.

Finally he stopped for his own sake. He took his hand off his privates and, shifting around behind his back,

130

located his cigars and the matches. He knew where they were because he'd been careful to keep them on his right side away from the side where he'd sluiced himself off with water. He wanted a drink, but he knew the whiskey was up near the chair, and he didn't feel as if he had the strength to drag Lily Gail up and back. He was also thirsty, but the water bucket was sitting off to his left and back. Again, it would involve moving Lily Gail, and she was beginning to weigh a ton.

His scrambling hands finally found his cigars and the little bundle of matches. Sitting up straight, in a bind because of the position his legs were in, he managed, by bending his head to the right and leaning down while he reached up as far as he could with his right hand, to get a cigar in his mouth. But lighting the match was a chore. Surprisingly, the tin tray Lily Gail had been feeding him from came to hand, and he was able to strike a match on that. With more difficulty he got the burning flame up to his cigar and lit it and got the smoke drawing. Then he shook the match out and dropped it.

Lily Gail said, "Now I reckon you are a-gonna go to burnin' me with that cigar."

She had her eyes open and was staring at him. Her face was a mess. It had been squashed and rubbed into the dirt and straw of the floor and was scratched and muddy. Her hair was tangled and a little blood was running out of her mouth. He assumed she'd either banged it against the floor or bit it while he was hurting her with his legs.

He gave her a look. The thought that his life rested on this ignorant, unreasonable, stubborn girl was as frightening as anything he'd ever run up against. Anyone with the common sense of an armadillo would have given in long ago. He could not understand her attitude. He said, "I hadn't thought of it in a while, but now that you mention it I might have to. I reckon it will hurt like fire."

"It ain't gonna make me he'p you. 'N if you don't be careful with them matches, you'll set this hay on fahr an' blow us both up with that dynamite yonder."

It suddenly put a thought into his head. She'd stood the pain because she knew he couldn't afford to go too far. She was no good to him dead. But what if he presented her with a situation over which he had no control? Say, setting fire to the straw and letting it burn toward the dynamite? Would she be so nonchalant about getting blown up? How would she view her end then?

He said, "Lily Gail, I'm gonna give you one more chance to help me. After that I'm going to give up."

"What you talkin' about?"

He shrugged. "You are right. If I kill you I won't help myself, so I got no reason to kill you. But if you won't help me I got no reason to live. But there's one thing I won't allow to happen and that is for the Gallaghers to get their hands on me. I'm sure they would make sure my death was long and drawn out. And I don't want them to beat me. You are my only hope, but you won't help. So, then, I guess we might as well both go down together."

Her face got a little more alert. "Whatever be you talkin' about?"

"How your insides feel?"

She gave him an ugly look. "You'd like me to say they killin' me. Wa'l, I ain't gonna give you that pleasure."

"Not at all," he said. "I was just going to tell you that you won't have to hurt much longer."

"What? What be you talking about?"

He didn't answer. Instead he struck another match with his right hand, quickly transferred it behind his back to his left, and then awkwardly flipped it out toward the haystack. It landed a couple of feet away and lay there burning for half a minute before it fizzled out.

She raised her head and looked to her left. She could see the thin smoke drifting into the air from the death of the match. She said, "Here! What are you playin' at?"

"Blowing us up," he said calmly. She suddenly started to struggle, but he caught her with his legs and clamped her in place. "Be still, Lily Gail. You wanted to be stubborn. Well, now we can both be stubborn."

He repeated the process with another match. She swiveled her head around, looking back, and they both watched as the match burned slowly and then, bit by bit, ignited the hay around it. It started with just the smallest fire, but in a moment it had begun to spread until it was covering an area some six inches wide, mostly moving toward where the hay was the thickest, which was toward the haystack because he'd cleared a lot of the hay away from his sitting and lying area.

Lily Gail said, alarm in her voice, "Are you crazy! You'll set that thar dynamite on fahr and blow us to kingdom come!"

She began making a real effort to free herself, jerking back and forth and pounding at him. He said, "What's the matter, Lily Gail? I thought you didn't care if I killed you."

"Not like this, you damn fool! Help! Help! Turn me loose so I can git to that water bucket! I got to put that thang out! Look how it is growin'!"

He knew something that she didn't know. He knew that about two feet further on the hay was wet where he'd taken his bath. The fire would never burn through that. He said, "You going to help me, Lily Gail? You going to get me the hay rake?"

"Swivel me round! Turn me round so's I can reach the water bucket. All I got to do is tip it over. Hurry, for Pete's sake!"

"You going to get that rake for me, Lily Gail?"

"Yes!" she yelled. "Jest hurry! We gonna git blowed up."

"You swear it!"

"Yes, yes, yes!"

"What? Swear it."

"I swear it. I swear I'll fetch the rake. Hell, I'll fetch you the keys you want me to. Only git me to that water bucket."

"Swear on Eugene's head."

There was a pause, but only for a second. "I swear on Eugene's head."

He turned so she could tip over the water bucket and put out the fire. As she did he said, "If you've lied won't be no more water buckets to use. Understand?"

Chapter 7

At the end of her reach her fingers slowly stroked the hay rake back toward her. Finally it rested in the palm of her hand. Longarm was in a terrific strain, his leg chain stretched as far as he could pull it. He had let her slip through his legs until he had her just around the knees. He watched as she held the rake handle in her hand, not moving to pull it in. He could almost hear her mind debating about finally, irrevocably throwing it out of reach.

He said softly, "I got plenty more matches, Lily Gail."

She hesitated for a second more, and then began pulling the rake toward her. As she did he began turning his body so that his back would be toward the front of the barn where her apron lay just eight or ten feet away. She kept pulling in the rake, the handle reaching him and then going by until he could finally grasp it with his hands. He said, "That's enough, Lily Gail. Now you just lay down and behave."

She said sullenly, "Whyn't you let me go. I don' like you seein' me nakid no more."

His heart was beating like a hammer. "Trust me, Lily Gail, I am not looking at you. Right now my mind is on something else."

With the rake in both hands he twisted his body to the right, which had the effect of dragging Lily Gail along with his legs, back toward the ridgepole.

It was as awkward as anything he had ever done, but holding the end of the rake with both hands over toward his right side, he lifted it up in the air and let it fall on the apron. It just did reach. The teeth were pointing downward and he slowly, very slowly began to pull the apron toward him. The hay was scattered, but he still feared the apron might be facing the wrong way and the keys might fall out and be lost in the straw. He pulled, hand over hand, on the rake, and slowly the apron came toward him. Just as he had it in reach Lily Gail suddenly summoned up strength and began to roll and wiggle and flail and kick. He clamped down on her knees with the calves of his legs with such pressure that she let out a high-pitched scream and collapsed. "Damn you!" he swore. "Damn you to Hell! You mess me up now I'll kill you for sure!"

Then he had the apron and he plunged his hand in the pocket. For a second his heart stopped. It was empty. But then he realized he'd just gotten to the first fold. It was a deep pocket and there, at the bottom, he felt the hard, metallic, lifesaving form of the keys. He let his breath out slowly.

It took him a moment to find the key for the manacles. First he freed his left wrist. His heart almost stopped when the rusty key seemed to hang in the rusty lock, but then it turned and the two-inch-wide steel band opened.

He freed his hand, feeling a surge of elation, and then awkwardly uncuffed his right hand. For just a second he flexed his shoulders, enjoying the feeling for the sheer freedom of it. But he wasn't free yet.

With some difficulty, because he was still holding Lily Gail between his legs, he managed to reach his left ankle and get to the padlock that held the chain to him. There were two keys and naturally the first one didn't fit. He had expected that, the way his luck was going, but it caused Lily Gail to make one more flurry. He was seriously thinking of knocking her out, but instead, he took the time to squeeze her hard one more time until she subsided. After that he was able to insert the last key, twist it, see the lock open, and finally watch the last restraint fall from his body.

He said, in almost a shout, "Hot damn!"

With his hand he rolled Lily Gail off his leg and stood up. She ended up on her back, staring at him with accusing eyes. "Well! I guess you are just proud as peaches of yourself. Take advantage of a poor innocent girl. Ruin my stockin's an' take ever' kind of advantage of me. You ought to be shamed of yoreself."

"Yeah, Lily Gail. I don't know why I didn't want to stay here chained up and let Rufus Gallagher come in here and burn me alive. I guess I'm just too mean to understand." He shoved the keys in his pocket, and then knelt down and snapped one of the manacle cuffs on Lily Gail's thin wrist. He had to take it to the last notch of the ratchet to get it to fit tight enough. Then he hauled her to her feet.

"Now you are a-lockin' me up!" she said. "Me that never done you no harm a-tall! Mister, you take the cake."

He peered at her. "Are you really that dumb or are you

just playacting? I can't believe that you don't know what you did was wrong."

"Huh!" She made a show of hiding her breasts with her free arm. "Not by my lights it wasn't wrong. An' you ain't never gonna have no more fun with me. Never! You jest think on that, Mister Deputy Marshal."

He picked her apron up and slung it at her. "Put that on. You are getting uglier by the minute." Then he looked around his all-too-familiar place of captivity to see if there was anything else he wanted to take in the house immediately. There was the whiskey, but Lily Gail had said there was plenty of that inside, along with cigars. For the time being what he most wanted to do was get his boots and his shirt and his gunbelt back on. The rest of it could wait, including an inspection of the dynamite. But first he had to get Lily Gail secured and out of trouble's way. He said, "Come on," and started to walk away. She stood her ground, her manacled wrist outstretched to the length of the chain that stretched to the other cuff he was holding. She said, "No, damn you!"

He shrugged. "Fine. I'll just drag you." Without a look backward he started across the barn. He heard a little scream and a thump, but he didn't bother to look back. She was a strain, but he figured it was harder on her to be dragged with that hard cuff digging into her wrist than it was for him to drag her. He took three steps, picked up the lantern, and started for the barn door. Behind him he could hear her screeching and hollering, and then the chain slackened up. He looked back. She was on her feet, reluctantly following him. She said, "I cuss yore name, Custis Long. You are the sorriest excuse fer a man I ever come acrost. I hope Rufus an' them cut yore toes and fingers off one at at time."

He gave her an amused look and let her out of the barn, holding the lantern aloft to guide his way.

They went in through the kitchen, a room he'd never seen, and from there into the bedroom. Her bedstead was a big iron affair, and he dragged her across the room to the head of her bed and then locked the other cuff around the curved iron top of her bedstead. The bed was sturdy and, unless she could drag a hundred pounds or so, she wasn't going anywhere. But it also allowed her to lie down in the bed and gave her a little freedom, enough to reach the chamber pot if she needed to.

He saw her blue frock and her camisole and step-ins on a chair, and he picked them up and threw them at her. There was also a flannel nightgown draped over a bureau. He pitched that on the bed, then said, "Now, where are my clothes and my guns?"

She was sitting on the side of the bed. She said, "Don' you wisht you knew."

He shrugged. "I'll find them. I'll bring you some water in a few minutes and anything else you want. But my advice to you is to stay quiet and not kick up a ruckus. I don't want to hurt you, Lily Gail, but I'll knock you out if you make me."

"*Don' wan' to hurt me*. Now that there is a laugh." She put her free hand on her stomach. "My insides feel like they been run over by a bull. You are a mean man, Custis Long, and my happiness is knowin' the trouble you be in fer when Rufus an' them git back."

"Think what you want," he said. He set the lantern down on a bureau at the end of the room, and then carefully cleared Lily Gail's area of anything she could throw. When he was through he surveyed the situation. She was as tightly and safely held as he could manage on such short notice. But the important thing right

139

then, he thought, was to get ready for the arrival of the Gallaghers. He turned around and walked out of the room.

There was a lantern burning in the kitchen, and he used that to locate the one in the parlor and light it. After that he found his shirt and socks, and his belt, gunbelt, and carbine. They had all been placed neatly on a chair that sat in a big closet. Within a few moments he was dressed and had his weapons at hand. The derringer had been discovered in the big, concave silver buckle on his gunbelt and removed, but it was also in the closet and it was the work of a minute to get it back in place.

After that he stalked through the house, finding whiskey, matches, and cigars in the kitchen and several boxes of .44-caliber ammunition in the second bedroom, which had some men's clothes hanging in a chiffonier. He assumed they belonged to Emmett or some other member of the Gallagher gang.

Once he was rigged out he checked his revolver, found that it was still loaded, and then checked his carbine, easing the lever out a little so that the ejection port slipped back enough to see the cartridge in the chamber.

Finally he put his hat on. He felt nearly himself again. On a thought he checked his pockets. He'd had about seventy-five dollars in cash. It was gone. Emmett, he thought. Well, he'd just have to get that later.

He wondered at the time, and then realized his watch was still missing. He went into Lily Gail and asked her, but she gave him a spiteful look and said, "Don't you wish you knew." She'd taken off her stockings, but she hadn't bothered with the nightgown or her clothes. All she was doing was sitting on the side of the bed naked.

To find his watch he began opening bureau drawers and throwing their contents on the floor. "Here!" Lily Gail yelled. "You cut that out and right now!"

"Then tell me where my pocket watch is."

She sulked for a moment, but then said, "It's in the pantry cupboard in the kitchen. Emmett woulda taken it jest like he took yore money if I hadn't hid it. Though I don' expect no thanks from the likes of you."

"Thanks," he said.

He found the watch where she said it would be. The time surprised him. It was almost eleven o'clock. Assuming Lily Gail had come to him around eight, they'd passed three hours somehow in retrieving a hay rake to get an apron to get the keys. It just hadn't seemed that long.

Finally he found a bottle of whiskey, a glass, and a couple of cigars and some matches, and sat down at the kitchen table and poured himself out a drink. What he had to do now, he thought, was to assume that the Gallaghers would be coming and soon, and figure some kind of plan to stop them and contain them, and if he couldn't, to kill or capture as many as he could.

He had the alternative of riding to town to get the help of Kyle Greenwood and his deputies, but it was ten miles and, even riding hard, by the time he got Kyle and Kyle got his men rounded up, five or six hours could have passed. In the meantime the Gallaghers could arrive, discover he had escaped, take their dynamite, and leave.

No, he had to devise a plan where he could take them on alone and have some fair chance. Of course he didn't know how many of them there would be, and he had no way of guessing. If they were coming just for him there wouldn't be many. But if they were also planning to blow up the Lawton bank, then there would be a considerable number, perhaps a dozen, perhaps twenty.

He couldn't hope to handle or capture, or even protect himself against, that many men. And he wasn't on a good horse, so he couldn't wait to see what the odds were like and then light out if they weren't to his liking.

He sat there, sipping at his whiskey and puffing on his cigar, thinking, going over all the pluses and minuses. Of course his biggest plus was that they wouldn't be expecting trouble. They'd think he was still chained in the barn. And another big plus was the dynamite, though he was damned if he knew how he was going to put it to use.

He knew about dynamite. An army demolitions engineer had given him a course on handling the stuff and how to make it work for you. But if you wanted to blow someone up you had to get them near enough to the stuff to have it do its job. Besides, he didn't know exactly what was under the hay. There might just be dynamite with no fuse caps or fuse cord or detonators of any kind. Without detonators dynamite wasn't a hell of a lot of use. He'd heard stories of men setting it off with a rifle bullet, but the army engineer had said that was all so much bullshit. He'd said if the dynamite was old and if some of the nitroglycerin had began to leak out, it got unstable and such a thing could happen. But fairly new dynamite was as stable as a log without a detonator.

He finished his drink and poured another. Obviously, then, the first thing he needed to do was go out in the barn and take a survey of what was on hand. He really couldn't do any planning until he was certain of what tools he had.

What would be handy, he thought, was if he had a messenger he could send into Wichita Falls to summon Kyle Greenwood and some men. He smiled as he thought of approaching Lily Gail with the idea. One thing for sure, he'd probably hear some cussing like he'd never heard before.

He sat there thinking about her, a bemused smile on his face. The damn woman had put him in as tight a spot as he'd ever remembered being in. And done it just as slick as any addle-headed, scatter-brained ignoramus was capable of doing. He decided then and there that it wasn't just the smart ones you had to watch out for. A person as dumb as Lily Gail was almost brilliant in her ignorance.

The thought of time passing, time he might need later, suddenly roused him. He finished his drink, and was on the point of going out to the barn when he became aware of a low moaning coming from the bedroom. He went in to find Lily Gail doubled over and rocking back and forth. He said, "What the hell's the matter with you?"

She turned a tear-stained face up to him. "You a fine one to ast. You like to have killed me is what's the matter." She rubbed her middle. "I just hurt all over, expecially round my middle."

"What did you do with that laudanum?"

She got a wary look in her eyes. "We used it all up on you."

"C'mon, I don't believe that. You neither one of you had the slightest idea how much it would take. Where's the other bottle?"

She looked sullen. "I ain't gonna tell you. You jest lookin' fer a reason to kill me. I'd go to sleep an' never wake up."

He was impatient. He still had the barn to reconnoiter. He said, "I'm not as dumb as you and Emmett. I know how to use the stuff. Besides, if I was going to kill you I already would have. I'm going to need you. Now unless you want to go on hurting, tell me where the laudanum is."

She looked sulky. "Kitchen."

"In the pantry? Where my watch was?"

"I furget."

He went into the kitchen, and soon found a little bottle of the drug. The label on the clear bottle with the clear liquid in it had a skull-and-crossbones symbol, which was the universal warning of the pharmaceutical trade that something was dangerous.

He unscrewed the bottle and smelled it. It was laudanum all right. Then he rummaged around until he found a big tablespoon and went back in to Lily. She was sitting as he'd left her. He poured out a level tablespoonful of the clear liquid and held it out to her mouth. "Take it."

She glanced up at him. "I don' trust you."

"Then don't take it," he said. "Hell, I don't care one way or the other."

"Well . . . all right," she said. She opened her mouth and moved her head and the spoon disappeared. She swallowed, licking her lips. "That stuff tastes pretty good. Kind o' sweet."

He poured out another tablespoonful. "Take one more and then turn around and lay down. You don't want this stuff to knock you out sitting on the side of the bed."

She took the second dose and then dutifully turned around and lay down. She said, "If you've kilt me you can't take no satisfaction 'cause I don't kere. Rufus will be comin' fer you."

"I'll be here," he said.

She looked surprised. "You ain't fixin' to take off?"

He shook his head. "Not if I have any hopes of catching some of the worst bandits in the territory. For a change I won't have to be hunting them down."

She drooped her head. He could already see the laudanum beginning to work by the glaze that was coming over her eyes. "You must be loco," she said.

"You don't want to put your gown on?"

"It's too damn hot," she said.

It was amazing, he thought. She was lying there naked and yet nothing stirred inside him. It was as if, now that he was free of the bonds that she had controlled, he was free of her. She was still a very good-looking woman, but the wild lust he had felt was gone. Now she just looked shopworn and tired and drugged. Before he left she asked for some water, and he went into the kitchen and found a glass and brought it to her. But by the time he got back her eyes were closed and she was asleep. He gently put the glass down on the bedside table and then left the bedroom, taking the kerosene lantern with him as he went.

He picked up another lantern in the kitchen and let himself out the back door. There was no point in trying to be careful or quiet, not carrying two lanterns in the middle of a black night. If there was anybody out there he was already a splendid target and they'd have to be blind to miss him.

He went into the barn. The horse nickered at him immediately, and he realized that the animal hadn't been fed that day. He went across to where the cavalry horse was tied. There was plenty of water in a barrel, but the horse's feed trough was empty. He took a big scoop and transferred some feed from a sack to the trough. The horse immediately began eating, not paying him any more mind than if he'd been part of the furniture. He reckoned cavalry horses didn't get too attached to human beings. All a man represented to a cavalry horse, probably, was a lot of work and trouble in the hot sun.

He thought that he should move the horse, maybe put him out in the little corral where Lily Gail had her buggy horse. Then he decided he'd better make an inspection of the dynamite before he did anything else.

He found the hay rake. It felt surprisingly light now that he was handling it without chains. He left one of the lanterns hanging from a peg in the ridgepole he'd been chained to, and then cautiously took the other closer to the haystack. He set it on the floor about six feet back from the hay and began carefully pulling the hay away from the various boxes.

It was a bigger stash than he had expected. There were eight cases of dynamite with forty-eight sticks to the case, enough, he figured, to level a small town. There were two cases of .44-caliber ammunition and a case of Winchester Model 73 lever-action repeating carbines. There were two small boxes of detonator caps and a small plunger-operated detonator, along with a wheel of rubber-coated detonating wire that could be attached to the plunger box on one end and the dynamite on the other. The markings on the tin wheel the wire was rolled on said there was two hundred feet of wire.

He stood there studying the explosives, thinking. He had several different ways to take on the Gallaghers. The trick was to pick the right one the first time, because one time was all he was going to get. He got out his watch and looked at it. It was past midnight.

The first thing he thought he ought to do was secure the horse at a little distance from where the trouble might occur. He left the explosives uncovered, went over to the cavalry horse, saddled and bridled him, and then, with a coil of rope over his shoulder, walked himself and the horse out into the dark night by a back door to the barn. He walked about a hundred yards until he found a small oak tree. He tied the horse's reins to the saddlehorn, took the bits out of the horse's mouth, and then put him on about a fifty-foot picket rope so the animal could graze. He didn't know if he was going to need the horse or not, but if he did, he was going to need it mighty bad.

After that he went back to the little corral just behind the barn, caught up Lily's little buggy horse, and took him in the barn. He looked around until he'd found a bridle for the horse, and then he took the horse and, somewhat against the horse's wishes, led him into the house, turning him loose in the living room. He figured that would upset Lily Gail no end, having a horse in her living room, but he didn't think she'd mind so long as she was asleep, and she'd probably be sleeping for some time.

There were three lanterns burning, and he put out two and carried the third into the kitchen. Then he sat down at the table with the bottle of whiskey and a cigar and set in to think matters out. He did not really expect the Gallaghers until sometime the next day, but he had no intention of being asleep when they arrived. He'd had plenty of time to rest while he'd been chained up in the barn, and he figured he could stay up for seventy-two hours if he had to.

His main problem was where did he want to locate himself. He could be out in the fields when they arrived. Or he could be in the house or the barn. If there were only three or four of them, he could handle them with a rifle and a pistol. But if, as he expected, there were a dozen or more, he wouldn't be able to kill or capture or disperse them all. He might be able to kill one of the Gallaghers with a first shot, but he calculated that that first shot was the only free one he'd get. Then he would be on the defensive.

He didn't want to be in the barn because of the dynamite. Besides, the barn would be harder to defend because there were fewer places to look out from.

That left the house. If he used the house, then he had to have some way to reduce the gang's numbers dramatically because he couldn't defend the house against a large group for more than an hour. The house was a frame structure, and he doubted that many of the walls would stop a bullet. The only advantage the house held was that it had a lot of windows and he could run from place to place and have a better idea what his enemy was up to.

His only practical method of seriously hurting the gang was with the dynamite. But how he was going to do that, get them in a position where he could use the dynamite, was something he hadn't figured out yet.

So he sat, drinking and smoking and thinking. At about two in the morning he came to a conclusion. The horse had come into the kitchen and was standing, staring at him. Longarm said, "I know you feel a little out of place, but I might need you in case I got to come out of here at a dead run. Of course you'll be doing the running."

The horse didn't answer back.

Longarm was about to get up and put the first part of his plan in motion when he heard a plaintive voice calling, "Help, help, help . . ." He took the lantern and followed it into the bedroom, where Lily Gail was chained to the iron bedpost. She was on her back, still naked. She stared at him with wide, frightened eyes. "I was scared," she said. "What is going on?"

"You've had some laudanum. You're a little drugged. You'll be all right in a moment."

148

She rattled the manacle that was attached to her right wrist. "Why you got me chained up like this? I thought we wuz lovers."

"We ain't lovers. And I got you chained up because the Gallaghers are coming and I don't want you sticking a knife in my back while I'm watching for them."

Her eyes were big and round. "I dreamt a horse come in here. I could see him plain as day."

"That wasn't a dream. I got a horse in the house. Your buggy horse."

She stared at him. "You ain't got no right to brang no horse in my house. He'll make a mess all over the place."

"That," he said, "is the last thing I'm worrying about. I need that horse in here in case I have to get out fast."

"The Gallaghers ain't here yet?"

"No. Was you expecting them?"

She looked off toward the window. "I jest wish they'd hurry. I hope they hang you. Put a rope round yore neck and put you on a horse. I want to be the one slaps the horse out from under you."

"You are just a little darlin', ain't you?" He turned to go.

"I'm scairt of the dark. You got to leave me some light."

He stared at her. "Why the hell should I do anything for you? You just got through saying how much you'd like to hang me."

She got the look on her face that he remembered. "You leave me a light you kin come in whenever you want 'n look at me." As if to emphasize the point she spread her legs slightly.

He laughed, but without humor. "Lily Gail, you are the last thing I got on my mind. I can promise you that."

She spread her legs more and put her free hand between her legs, saying in her purring voice, "Don't tell me you don' like to look at this. Here, see it? I bet you can see the pink."

He was unmoved. "That doesn't work anymore, Lily Gail. All that is over with. I'll leave you a lamp, but that's just because I believe you really are afraid of the dark."

He set the lamp down on top of the bureau that was at the other end of the room from her, and then went to the two windows and carefully pulled together the heavy curtains so that no light would shine out and no one could see in. "Wouldn't want any of your kin peeking in at you," he told her.

She flared up. "You are just a dirty dawg! They gonna take little pieces outten you and feed them to the hawgs. You gonna git yores, Mister Smart Aleck Deputy Marshal."

He paid her no more mind, but went back in the kitchen, now having to feel his way in the dark. He bumped into the horse, who was standing in the kitchen door, and then had to sidle by the animal before he could get to the table and light another lantern.

The kitchen was the only part of the house that was made out of stone. That wasn't uncommon since the kitchen was the hottest room in the house and the stone walls kept it cooler. There was a trapdoor in a corner. He raised it and saw it went down to a very small cool cellar where potatoes and onions and other produce were stored and where meat was hung. He thought of putting Lily Gail down there just in case the Gallaghers tried to set fire to the house, but the trapdoor was made of wood and wouldn't provide much protection if they fired the house and the roof fell into the kitchen.

150

He took time to stoke up the embers in the stove and add a little wood. The big coffeepot had a little liquid left in it, but he threw it out, pumped in some fresh water, and threw in a handful of ground coffee that he found in the tray of the coffee mill. He didn't particularly want any coffee, but he thought he ought to drink a cup or two just to stay awake.

His watch said it was nearly four in the morning. He didn't have too much time left, not if they showed up as early as first light. He sat at the table, waiting for the coffee to boil, sipping whiskey and wishing he knew of some way to get word to Kyle Greenwood.

But there just wasn't any, so he figured to content himself with the job at hand and how best to make it come out his way. He knew he was probably going to be taking on odds that ought to be left alone. He knew if he had any sense he'd ride for town that instant and fetch back Greenwood and a dozen men. That would be the smart thing to do. But occasionally, according to Billy Vail, he didn't always do the smart thing. And besides, he couldn't bear the thought of having a shot at the Gallaghers and letting them slip away.

The horse was back, and he got up and took the reins loose from where they were tied behind the horse's neck, and then hitched the animal to a leg of the cast-iron stove. The kitchen, with its stone walls and big, heavy door at the back, was probably the best place to keep the horse safe from bullets that would be flying through the walls and the windows.

He could hear the faint voice of Lily Gail calling to him, but he ignored her and stood, thinking, wondering if there was anything else that needed tending before he got on with the main business out in the barn.

And that wasn't a business he was particularly anxious to get on with. True, he'd had that lesson from that army engineer, but dynamite was still dynamite and it was too much like women for his tastes. Like women, it could be just as docile and nice as a milk cow, and like women, it could blow up in your face for no seeming reason at all.

The coffee boiled, and he poured out a cup and put a little whiskey in it, and then stood there by the side of the table, sipping at the coffee and puffing on a cigar. There were some things a man didn't mind delaying, but this was one that wasn't going to get any better by delaying. A river might go down if you waited long enough, and a forest fire might burn out if you gave it time, but handling the dynamite wasn't going to change with any amount of time.

Finally he drank off the most of his coffee and set the cup back down, turned and walked to the heavy door, opened it, shoved the screen door back, and then, holding the lantern high, walked to the barn.

There was another lantern just inside the barn door, hanging on a peg, and he took a moment to light that one and hang it on a nail driven into his old ridgepole. As he hung the lantern he looked down, seeing the debris left from his confinement. He was lucky, and he knew it, now that he had the freedom and the chance to meet the Gallaghers in a way they wouldn't expect. Of course, he thought, that wasn't going to make the job any easier, and he knew he was a damn fool for sticking around when he could be miles from the place. But there it was, he was who he was and there was nothing he could do about it.

Holding the second lantern in his hand, he walked over and looked at the boxes of dynamite, cartridges, and detonators and the detonating cord and plunger box. He didn't hesitate long. His big jackknife was still in his pocket and he used the big blade to pry open the top of one of the boxes of dynamite.

There they were, the biggest firecrackers in the world. He took one up and leaned down to the lantern to have a close look at it. It looked new. At least none of the nitroglycerin had leaked through. That meant he didn't have to be more careful than he was already being. He put the stick back carefully, and then took down the roll of rubber-coated wire and the box of detonators and set them on the floor. He opened the little box of detonators and took up two of the deadly little instruments.

It was time to go to work in earnest.

Chapter 8

He took up a stick of dynamite and crimped a detonator into its end. He would only prime two sticks because that was more than enough. When they exploded there would be a very slight hesitation—about as long as Lily Gail could keep her mind on a subject, he thought to himself—and then the rest of the whole pile would explode.

He crimped a second detonator into the second stick of dynamite. That was just for insurance in case one detonator, for some reason, might be a dud. After that he pulled about six feet of cord off the reel and using his jackknife, stripped off the rubber coating, leaving the twisted copper wire bare. He unraveled the twist for about a foot, and then took one of the small wires that made up the twist and rammed it through the detonator and deep into the first stick of dynamite. He did the same with the second stick, and then, to be sure, crimped another detonator into a third stick of dynamite and rammed a wire deep into it. After that he laid the three sticks carefully back into the box, and took one wrap around the case to make sure the detonating cord wouldn't pull the loaded sticks out.

Now he found a short hoe, stuck the handle through the middle of the cord reel, and began backing toward the barn door, playing out the detonating cord as he went.

At the door of the barn he found a little clearance and shoved the cord under that, and then, avoiding the worn path, unreeled the cord through the tall grass on the side of the path to the back door. He reached back, pulled the screen door open, and then backed into the kitchen. As soon as he got inside he could hear Lily yelling her head off, but he paid her no mind.

When he was in the middle of the kitchen he stopped and set the cord reel on the floor. Better than half of the black rubberized cord had been unwound from the reel.

He went back out into the barn and carefully pulled the hay back over the stored explosives and ammunition. He didn't expect anyone to come looking around, but he wanted to take every precaution possible.

All that was left now was the little plunger box with its screw contacts on top. He took that and carried it to the door of the barn and set it down. Then he went back and walked along the line of detonator cord, carefully covering it with some of the loose hay that covered the floor.

When he had that done to his satisfaction, he picked up the plunger box and went back into the house. For a few minutes he looked around, and soon realized that if he blew up the barn with all those cases of dynamite in it, he'd want to be as far from it as possible. And that was somewhere near the front of the house. There was the cold cellar, but he couldn't see out of there and he would have to be able to see out to know when to ram the plunger home.

As he unrolled wire, heading through the kitchen and through the parlor, he wondered what kind of an explosion that much dynamite would make. Would he even be safe in the house? The truth was he didn't really know. He'd fired off dynamite a stick at a time, and had been awed by its power. But eight cases? He had no earthly idea what kind of a blast such an amount would produce. For all he knew it would blow up the barn and send the house flying like so much kindling wood.

By the front door of the house he set the plunger box down beside the reel of cord. He took the cord up and, sawing with his jackknife, cut it in two. Then, with the end that ran out to the barn to the dynamite, he stripped off several ends of bare wire. There were two screw posts on top of the plunger. He took one wire, wrapped it around one of the posts, and then screwed a wing nut down on it to tighten it and make sure it was in contact with the electricity that would be generated when he raised the plunger and then drove it home.

He took the rest of the bare wires and wrapped them around the second post, and again tightened them down with the wing nut. He sat back. It was done. He got out his watch. It was a little after five. Now there was nothing to do but wait.

Lily's voice was getting hoarse, but she was still either calling for him or cursing. He considered going in and giving her a target for her malice, but he didn't feel up to it right then. Instead he went into the kitchen and poured himself a cup of coffee, sweetened it with a good dollop of whiskey, and sat down with a cigar and his thoughts. The horse looked around at him, and he said, "Yeah, I know you know you ain't supposed to be in the kitchen, but believe me, you might be glad later on." He thought the horse looked a little smarter than Lily Gail.

As dawn was showing signs of breaking he found another mug, filled it with coffee, and took it into the bedroom. Lily Gail was sitting on the side of the bed, her eyes red and tear-stained. She looked up as he came in and said, "Oh. It's jest you."

He walked over and set the coffee on the floor near her. She still was naked, but she still held no appeal for him. "Yeah, I happened to be in the neighborhood and thought I'd drop in," he said.

She gave him a sullen look. "You think you are so smart."

He backed up to where he could lean against the bureau. The lantern was flickering low, running out of fuel, but that was all right. It would be light within the half hour. "I reckon we are going to have some company today and I'm going to have a job for you," he told her.

She shot him a look. "You think I'm a-helpin' you, you got 'nother thang comin'."

He shrugged. "You can call out from the house or you can call out from the barn. Makes me no difference. Might make a difference to you, though, because the barn is gonna be on fire."

She suddenly looked horrified. "You wouldn't!"

"Like hell I wouldn't," he said.

"You low-down dawg! You dirty sonofabitch!"

He shrugged. "Lily Gail, pretty soon it is going to dawn on you that I don't much care what your opinion of me is and you'll save yourself a lot of breath."

She looked at him suspiciously. "What you mean, call out?"

"To Rufus, to Emmett, to the Gallaghers. To them folks you're so close to."

"An' what am I supposed to call out?"

"You are going to tell them I'm in the barn."

She narrowed her eyes at him. "Why would I want to tell them somethin' like that?"

"Because I don't want them to know I'm in the house."

"How come?"

"So I can make my escape while they are looking in the barn," he lied.

She thought about it for a moment. "How come you don't just up and make yore escape now?"

"Because I wouldn't know which way to ride. Sure as I ride north that would be the way they are coming and I'd run smack into them. Same for the south. Or the east or west."

She leaned down, picked up her coffee, and sipped at it for a moment. "An' that's all you want me to do— call out to 'em?"

"Yes. Except I want you to make it seem kind of urgent so they'll all go straight to the barn. I don't want a couple of them coming in the house."

She sipped at her coffee and thought. "What you going to do to me if I won't do it?"

"I told you. Put you in the barn and, when I see them coming, set the barn on fire. *That* will take them straight to the barn."

"But they's all that dynamite." She stopped and stared at him. "You got a plan, ain'cha? An' it's got to do with that there dynamite. You plannin' on blowin' up Emmett an' them."

He shrugged. "If I have to set fire to the barn, yes, I guess it'll blow up."

A look of horror crossed her face. "An' me in it?" She made a little scream and put her hand over her mouth.

When she took it away she said, "Why, I'd be blowed to bits. My soul wouldn't never be together again. You'd be condemin' me to wander heaven in parts." Her face wore a look of horror.

He was mildly surprised at her reaction, but he didn't let it show. "That's up to you," he said.

"You wouldn't do that to a body! You be a lawman. A peace officer."

"Lily Gail, you keep talking about Rufus coming. What about Clem and Vern? Ain't they all together?"

She put both her hands over her mouth. "I ain't talkin' 'bout *them.*"

"Well, did Emmett just go to get Rufus? Is he the only one going to rob the Lawton bank?"

She just shook her head with her hands over her mouth.

"Where did Emmett have to go to get them? Oklahoma City? Hell, Lily Gail, I need some idea when they're gonna be here."

She took her hands away from her mouth. "You stop starin' at me with the slobber runnin' outta yore mouth. I ain't yores fer the takin' no more."

He gave her a look of disgust. "Can't you think about anything else, Lily Gail?" He looked around the room until he found the blue dress she'd had on the day before. He handed it to her. "Put that on."

She shook her manacled hand. "How'm I suppose to put this on over these here chains you got me bound up with? Reckon the bed will fit inside the dress?"

He sighed, took out the keys, and unlocked the manacle around her wrist. "You want me to find your small things? Your camisole and whatnot?"

She was getting into the dress, buttoning it up the front. "You ain't never to touch them thangs again.

'N you kin jest git out of my bedroom."

When she had the dress on, he caught her wrist before she could begin to cut up and latched the manacle back around it. She said in a whiny voice, "But I'm hongry."

"So am I. But I don't see nothing to eat."

"Let me loose 'n I'll whomp us up some bacon and aigs an' biscuits."

He said suddenly, "They're hiding out on the Kiowa reservation up north of here, near the Kansas line. That'd be just about the right distance. That's right, ain't it, Lily Gail?"

She fluffed at her hair with both hands. "I do not know what you are a-talkin' 'bout. An' I wisht you'd keep yore thinkin' to yoreself."

"Yes," he said. "They have bought their way onto that reservation and they are hiding out amongst the Kiowas. I'd bet my shirt on it. Nobody goes on that reservation. Not the cavalry, not federal officers. Nobody. Because the Kiowas have such a good reputation for policing themselves. That's where the Gallaghers are."

She gave him a look. "Fine lot 'o good it'll do you."

"Emmett rode to Lawton and took the train up there, taking his horse in a stock car. They'll come back the same way. What time does the first train from the north get into Lawton, Lily Gail?"

"You kin suck aigs for all you'll get outta me."

He went out of the bedroom, into the parlor, and to the front door. It was good daylight. A town the size of Lawton would have a train getting in early for the convenience of the businessmen who wanted to get in, get his business tended to, and then take a late afternoon train out. Longarm's watch said it was ten after six, and he was willing to bet that a train had already arrived or was about to.

He went back into the bedroom and gave Lily Gail another tablespoon of laudanum. She didn't want to take it. "I ain't hurtin' no more. What I want with that stuff for?"

"You'll start hurting when you get up and get to ginning around. Just take it."

Of course he was just giving it to her to keep her slightly dopey and not thinking too well. He unlocked her manacle from the iron bedstead, led her into the kitchen, and fastened it to the pipe part of the water pump that pumped water into the sink.

She said, "What is that damn horse doin' in my kitchen? Damn, a horse ain't supposed to be in the kitchen."

Longarm said, "You got any bread baked, Lily Gail? Anything we can eat won't be no trouble?"

"You turn me loose an' I'll fix us somethin' fine."

"Yeah, while you are running up the road to meet the Gallaghers."

She gave him an impish look. "Why, Marshal, I do declare I don't know who you be talkin' 'bout."

"Is there anything down in the root cellar we can eat quick? You got a smoked ham down there?"

She gestured at the oven of the big sooty wood stove. "They is some day-ol' biscuits in thar. If yore teeth is good—" She stopped as she saw the black rubber detonator cord running from the back door through the kitchen and on toward the front door. "What in the world is that? Some kind of wahr?"

"Something like that," he said. He very much hoped she would not recognize the wire and the detonator box for what they were. "You say there are biscuits in the oven?"

He pulled back the lid and found a big tray with a half dozen big, fluffy-looking baking-soda biscuits waiting.

He took the tray out and set it on the table and tried a biscuit. It was stale, but it was something to eat. Lily's tether allowed her just enough slack to sit down at the table with one hand free. He poured them both a fresh cup of coffee, added a little whiskey to his, and then broke a biscuit in half, soaked it in his coffee for a few seconds, and started gnawing away.

Lily Gail said, "You ain't got no more manners'n a blue-nosed mule."

But she too dipped the biscuit in her coffee, allowed it to soak, and then worried off a bite with her teeth.

He did not give them long to eat. After they'd finished a cup of coffee and a few biscuits, Longarm unlocked Lily Gail from the water pump and led her into the parlor to the front door. He got them both down on the floor, making sure that his carbine was near to hand, and cracked the door just enough to see out. The scenery hadn't changed much since he'd come down that same road. It seemed as if it had been ten or twelve years ago. But it was the same flat land waiting to bake under a summer sun and the same cloudless light blue sky. It was a half mile to the main road, but he could occasionally see a horseman passing by in one direction or the other.

Lily Gail pointed at the plunger box he'd put in the corner by the door. "What's that? That wahr leads right into it."

He said, "That's dangerous. You touch that and you could lose a finger and maybe a hand." He looked into her eyes, trying to see if she looked any more stupid than usual. She moved a little slower, it seemed to him, and talked a little slower. He supposed the laudanum had done its work, but he wished he'd given her two tablespoons. "Lily Gail, I figure it won't be long until

Emmett and whoever he's brought will be riding up to the house. Now you are to do exactly as I say."

"Why?"

"Because if you do, I'll be able to get away and then I'll help get Eugene out of prison. You understand?"

"Aw, you're just funnin' me."

"Yeah, but what if I'm not? You willing to take a chance on not helping Eugene?"

She looked at him pensively. "What you want me to say?"

"I want you to yell out to Emmett that I'm in the barn. I want you to yell out for them to hurry because I'm having some kind of fit, foaming at the mouth and you don't know what all."

She squeezed her face up. "What? Why, that's crazy."

"You just do it. You just tell them to hurry around to the barn if they want to find me alive. Tell them you're scared to go."

"They ain't gonna believe me."

"You just do what I tell you and you won't have no trouble."

"What you gonna do if I don't?"

He had been holding the loose end of her manacle, and now he took it and locked it around the inside knob of the front door. He said, "I'm not going to do anything to you, but then they'll probably catch me and I won't be able to go and help Eugene get out of jail."

She pulled her head back. "Aw, I ain't believin' you gonna do any such thang. Who you think you funnin'?"

Damn, he thought, he should have given her maybe three tablespoonfuls of the dope. "All right, Lily Gail, then you ain't gonna leave me any choice. Do you remember what I told you I'd do to you before? If you didn't do what I said?"

She looked at him, her eyes clearing a little. She said slowly, "Now, you didn't mean that."

"You watch me," he said. He started getting out the keys from his pocket. "I'll chain you in the barn just as sure as you're born and set it on fire when I first set eyes on them. Then it will be your guess if they can get you out of there before the fire burns you up or gets to the dynamite. Course they might decide to chase me and forget all about you. What do you think, Lily Gail? You want to risk it?"

Fright had cut straight through the fog caused by the laudanum. She said, "Never mind, never mind! I'll do what you say! I'll do anything you say! Jest don't chain me in thar' with all that dynamite!"

"I have your word on that?"

"Yes, my goodness, yes! I don't want to be blowed all to little pieces."

"You ain't doing this for Eugene then?"

"The hell with Eugene. You jest don't put me in that barn."

He put his head back and laughed.

He had calculated it would take them about an hour to get off the train, get organized, and then ride toward the ranch. Allowing another two hours for the ride, he'd calculated they should be showing up sometime between nine-thirty and ten o'clock. He looked at his watch just after he spotted the large party of men coming down the main road from Lawton. It was ten minutes until ten. He reckoned they were just about on time.

He watched, half hoping it wasn't them because of the size of the party, but sure enough, they turned in on the little road that led to Lily Gail's house. He couldn't make an accurate count, but he judged there to be somewhere between twelve and fourteen men. He let his breath out in a long sigh. He really had bitten off a pretty good mouthful. Everything had better go just as he'd planned, or he was going to be in a world of trouble. He leaned down to Lily Gail, who was slumped against the side of the door, dozing. "Wake up. They are coming. Wake up."

She sat up and looked around. "Huh?"

He cracked the door a little more. "Take a look. Here they come."

She cautiously put an eye around the door and peered outside. Then she said, "Oh, my! Jest look at 'em. And they is Rufus right up in the front. Oh, don't they look grand."

"Is Clem or Vern with them?"

But she was too busy with her own thoughts. "My, look at 'em! I bet ol' Emmett is jest proud as a peacock to be ridin' with that bunch."

The men had pulled their horses down from a trot to a slow walk as they approached the house. Longarm could see that Rufus was still a little in front with Emmett riding just to his left. He saw Rufus turn and say something to Emmett and the man nod and point toward the back of the house. Longarm guessed he was pointing toward the barn where the prisoner was supposed to be. Now that they were close he tried for a quick count, and figured they numbered fourteen. Again, that was bad odds for one man, especially a man handicapped by a silly woman.

They were near now, almost to the little hitching rail that Longarm had first tied his horse to on that unsuspecting day that seemed so long ago. Between him and them there was just the little narrow porch, a strip of ground to the hitching rail, and a few yards. As they came up to the house he wondered if they would dismount or call out from their saddles instead.

He raised Lily Gail up so that she was standing just behind the door with her face near the crack in the door. He switched over to the other side, his back to the wall. He drew his revolver. He waited. He could hear the men outside talking to each other, their voices just a mumble of sound.

He hissed at Lily Gail, "Remember, tell them I'm in the barn. Tell them to hurry. You better do it right."

She put her knuckles to her mouth and bit at them. "It ain't right. It just ain't right. They be kin."

He said fiercely, "They're not kin, damnit. Do what I tell you."

Outside a voice—Longarm guessed it was Emmett— yelled, "Lily Gail! Lily Gail! Whar are you, girl?"

"Now!" Longarm said. "Now!"

She pulled the door back and looked out at them. Her left arm was still chained to the door knob. She opened her mouth and then closed it. She opened it and yelled, "He ain't in the barn! He's here! Ya'll run!"

"Sonofabitch!" Longarm said. He shoved Lily Gail out of the way and swung around the door jamb, his revolver stretched out and searching for the face of Rufus with his big mustache. He caught a glimpse as the men were backing their horses and wheeling them around. He fired, but saw that another figure had come between him and his target. It was Emmett, and Longarm saw the bullet strike the man in the side of the chest and knock him sideways off his horse. He fired again into the horseman in front, and another man fell slowly off the side of his horse. He got in one more shot, but then the return fire was starting and bullets were whistling through the door.

He ducked down and raced past the door, grabbing his carbine as he did, and ran into the second bedroom, the front one. There were two windows on the side and he knocked out a glass. The men were riding into the open fields, too far for his revolver. He fired at the hindmost man and saw him pitch forward out of his saddle, hang in the stirrup of his running horse for a few strides, and then break loose and go rolling and tumbling over the prairie. He levered in another cartridge and fired at another figure, but the range was increasing and they were cutting back to his left.

He ran out of the bedroom and into the kitchen to see what kind of shot he could get out of the small window at the back. He caught sight of two horsemen running their horses four hundred yards away. He fired, but he knew he'd missed them.

He also knew he was in for a hell of a hard time. There were at least nine, maybe ten heavily armed, highly capable men out there who now wanted him dead. He walked slowly back into the living room to collect Lily Gail and get her in a safe place.

As he did the bullets started whizzing through the thin walls and windows of the house.

Chapter 9

He brought Lily and the detonator plunger box back to the kitchen. He put the detonator box down in the root cellar, but kept Lily Gail chained to the pump pipe and lying on the floor. Occasionally he would make a dash into the frame part of the house to fire a quick shot out at the men, who now had the house completely encircled. He didn't want them to think he was penned back in the kitchen. He could tell that they were slowly moving in, narrowing the distance between them and his puny firepower. When they rushed the house there'd be too many of them for him to cover at once.

His only hope was that some passerby who was headed for Wichita Falls would hear the gunfire and carry word to Kyle Greenwood. But he considered even that a very remote hope. The house was too far from the main road for bystanders to tell a gunfight was going on, and gunfire was a common occurrence in such country, too common to arouse much interest.

The horse was frightened. It kept nickering and rearing up as much as its short tether would let it. From the floor Lily said, "Git that damn horse outten here 'fore he steps on me."

Longarm was taking a quick look out the little kitchen window. He had the heavy wooden door at the back shut and barred. He said, "I got an idea I'm gonna need that horse before this is all over. I know damn good and well I don't need you."

The fight had been going on for about an hour. Every few minutes Longarm would go back to the side window in the kitchen, looking from the front side of the house and trying to see back toward the barn to see if any of the bandits had taken cover there. Sometimes he'd think he saw movement, but he knew it could be shadows. A few times he'd ventured into the parlor and looked out the windows on the other side of the house, the side that faced the big pasture. There was plenty to see out that side. He counted at least five men firing into the house from the tall grass. He couldn't see the men, just the faint puffs of white powder as they methodically worked the house over.

Back in the kitchen Lily Gail was lying on the floor trembling. "You got to let me go! One of them bullets is gonna hit me and then where will I be?"

Longarm said, "You should have thought of that."

She made a gesture toward the door to the root cellar. "Whyn't we at least git down there? They can't shoot us down there."

"I don't want to be stuck down there like a rat in a hole," Longarm said. He was busy turning the round wooden kitchen table on its side and rolling it over until it blocked the door to the parlor. It would provide some cover when they came in the front door, which they were almost sure to do when they got impatient. That or set fire to the house. He figured the only reason they hadn't done that was that he was holding Lily Gail.

He was reloading his carbine when a voice from outside yelled, "Lily Gail! Lily Gail! Girl, you ar'right?"

Longarm jumped to her side and put his hand over her mouth. He yelled back, "She's just fine, Gallagher. Why don't ya'll just get the hell out of here and let us go on with what we were doing."

The voice yelled back. "I want to hear from Lily Gail. Girl! Kin you hear me?"

She suddenly bit Longarm's hand. He jerked it away and, before he could stop her, she yelled, "Rufus, Rufus! You got to save me! Help, help!"

He didn't know if they had heard her or not. A voice shouted, "What? What's that you say, girl?"

Longarm held his hand over her mouth. He said, "You yell again and I'll knock you out. You understand?"

Just then a bullet came through the kitchen window and went ricocheting around the room. Before, the lead-nosed bullets had struck the stone walls and flattened themselves. But if the gang began using steel-nosed encased cartridges, the kitchen wouldn't be any safer than anyplace else.

Lily Gail was almost crying. "Le's, fer Gawd's sake, git in the root cellar. They can't shoot down there."

"No, but they can pour a gallon of kerosene through the trapdoor and then fling in a match." But even as he said it he knew he was going to have to do something.

With one hand he reached up and untied the horse. He ought to at least have a chance to survive on his own. Then he raised the trapdoor to the root cellar and looked inside. He'd seen a hundred just like it. It was about six feet deep, six feet wide, and six feet long, with shelves to hold canned goods and potatoes and strings of onions tied up to dry.

He crawled across the floor and unlocked the manacle holding Lily Gail to the pipe of the water pump. Then he shoved her toward the root cellar opening. She needed no urging. Within seconds she'd scuttled across the floor and down the wooden steps and was huddled in a corner of the little hole.

Longarm went down slower, pulling the trapdoor down shut after him. He had an idea, but he didn't have the slightest notion as to whether it would work or not. He had to try and get some kind of message to Kyle Greenwood, and he could think of only one way.

Once he was in the cellar he groped around until he found the plunger box. He didn't know how far eight cases of dynamite could be heard, but he was fixing to find out. He held the box between his legs and took the handle of the plunger in his hand. You had to screw the handle a few turns before it was free to be pulled up and then pushed down. It was a safety device, he'd been told. He unscrewed it and then pulled the handle up. He hesitated, wondering if Rufus and his men had found the cord and cut it or disarmed it in some way.

Lily Gail said, "What in the world are you doin'?"

He said sharply, "Be quiet!"

He listened. It seemed that the firing had stopped outside. He listened for a moment more. He could swear he could hear boot heels on a woooden floor. If he was right, they were in the house.

A voice said, "Lily Gail?"

172

He raised his shoulder up, raising the trapdoor. Two men were standing just beyond the wooden table. Without pause he had his revolver in his hand. He fired at the chest of the first man and then, without seeing him go over backward, shot the second one in the side as he began to turn.

Then he let the lid back down and plunged the lever home.

For a time he wasn't conscious of any noise other than his own breathing. It just seemed that the earth had suddenly decided to heave itself back and forth. That lasted for what seemed like a month or so, and then he heard a noise that was too loud for his ears to stand. He clapped his hands over them and knelt with his head between his knees. The noise seemed to go on and on and on. But over it, somehow he was conscious of someone screaming. He knew it wasn't him because he had his teeth clenched so hard his jaw muscles were aching. After a long time he became aware that it was Lily Gail. She was on top of his back with her arms wrapped around him and her mouth next to his hands. She was screaming like he'd never heard anyone scream before.

He didn't know how long it was before he came out of his daze. He began to hear voices. At first he thought they were inside his ringing head, but after a time he identified them as coming from overhead. Still, through the thick wood of the trapdoor, they were broken and hard to understand. Mostly what he caught at first were strings of cussing. Then a man said, "Sonofabitch has still got to be here. He could'na slipped past us an' he ain't plastered on what's left of the walls of this house."

He could hear movement and the noise of wood and debris being shoved around. Then a voice said, "Reckon they'd be down in that thar root cellar?"

There was quiet, and then a voice said, "I'd reckon, Rufus. What about Lily Gail?"

Somebody spit. "Don' know 'bout her. But I want me that sonbitch. Yank him outta thar."

"Might still be armed."

"Don' gimme no lip. Kick that trash offen that door an' lift it up."

Longarm and Lily Gail were wedged in at the very front of the cellar, down beside the steps. He held her back with his left hand, and edged out to where he could get a good view of the front when the door was lifted.

"I doan know I'm jest all that ready to yank up thet door. I'm tellin' you he would be armed."

"I want thet sonbitch. Do it, by Gawd, er I'll shoot you myself."

Longarm was ready when the first crack of light appeared as the door was lifted. When it was two inches open he could see a belly and a belt and the beginning of a man's upper body. He fired to hit just above the belt buckle. There was a yell and the door dropped back shut. Instantly Longarm jammed back into the corner pushing Lily Gail back, squeezing as far back away from any angle of fire that could be made through the door.

"Shoot in thar!"

"What 'bout Lily Gail?"

"Hell with Lilly Gail. Fahr in thar, I tell you."

A fusillade of shots rang out, and shafts of light suddenly pierced the black of the cellar from the holes in the trapdoor. By their light Longarm could see the mess of canned goods and broken jars of preserves and potatoes and all the other goods that had been jolted off the shelves by the force of the dynamite blast.

"Hell, Rufus, we ain't gonna hit him thet way."

"Then git some coal oil. We'll burn his ass out."

"Whar' we gonna git any coal oil?"

"In the barn. Hell, I don't know whar you gonna git some coal oil. One of ya'll pile a bunch of kinlin' on thet door and light it. It'll ketch."

"Whyn't you do it, Rufus? I'm willin' fer you to have the glory."

There was a silence.

"Ar'right, ar'right. Ain't no call to point thet pistol at me. I'm fixin' to do it."

Down in the cellar Longarm waited. The air should have been cooler, but it felt close and hot to him. Lily Gail was slumped back in the corner. By the light let in by the bullet holes Longarm could see her face. It was strained and drawn. Her eyes were wide open and round. She never seemed to blink. For a while he'd held his hand over her mouth, but since she'd heard Rufus say, "Hell with Lily Gail," she'd sat silent and shivering.

He was listening for the sound of a footstep of the top of the cellar door. He heard little thumps as small pieces of wood were thrown somewhere in the middle of the door. He wondered where they were getting all the "kindling" wood. Maybe the dynamite blast had also shattered the house. He cocked his freshly loaded revolver. They could throw the wood on the door, but some one was going to have to get close to light it.

He heard Rufus's voice. "Wa'l, go ahead and set it afahr. What're you waitin' on, the sun?"

Longarm paused for three counts and then, as rapidly as he could, he fired six shots in a semicircle toward the front of the cellar door. He'd moved a step to the back to do it so that his shots would angle up at as small a trajectory as he could manage. He heard a yell and then, as he was hurrying back to his corner, heard a thump on the overhead door as if a heavy body had fallen on it.

"Sonofabitch! He's still got a stinger in his tail. Ah'm stayin' back from thet damn door."

Rufus said, "Ar'right. We'll wait the ornery sonbitch out. One of ya'll stay here case the air get's a little close fer him down thar. Rest of us'll go round up the horses. They scattered all over hell and back."

Longarm did not like it in the cellar. He had never liked closed-in places, and he especially had never liked closed-in places where his enemies could maneuver and see and he was blind and restricted.

And he was tired. Until Rufus and his men had walked away to get up their horses and he'd been able to relax a little, he hadn't realized just how tired he was. Except for the drug-induced night he'd slept in the barn, he really hadn't had any good sleep since before he'd found Genuine Bob. Worse, he'd been worried as to how to get out of his chains, and then how to handle the men who were coming. After that had come the actual tension of the fighting. He didn't know when he'd last relaxed.

He squatted there in the semi-gloom of the cellar. A beam of light from a bullet hole was shining on his right shoulder. He glanced at it. It looked red. He frowned. He couldn't remember being hit, but maybe it was a wood splinter, though it was a powerful lot of blood for a wood splinter. He put his finger to the wet spot and tasted it. Tomato. He looked at the litter on the floor. He could see several broken jars of tomato preserves. He smiled. Apparently a bullet had hit one of the glass jars and it had exploded, blowing boiled tomatoes all over the place.

After he didn't know how long, he heard boot steps overhead. At least half a dozen men. He could hear snatches of conversation, but nothing that connected. Once he heard "Vern" and then something about him. He pricked up his ears, but didn't hear enough to make any sense.

He had loaded his revolver and discovered he had only five cartridges left in his shirt pocket where he carried his extras. His carbine was full, but that was only six more. He didn't have the ammunition to fight his way out and he had no way to make a getaway. He was boxed, trapped, caught. He cursed the day he'd decided to get in the cellar. He cursed the day he'd ever come to the damn ranch in the first place.

About the only thing he could figure to do was somehow wait until nightfall, and then slip out, kill as many as possible in the first few minutes, and gather up as many guns as he could. If there were only six or seven of them left he might have a chance. He'd more than likely have to eat some lead, but he might live through the fight.

Then, all of a sudden, he heard someone say loudly, "Hey! Look yonder. Who in hell be that a-comin'?"

A few minutes later he heard the sound of distant shots. Then he heard shots right over his head. A moment later he heard a shout, "Mount up! They's too many of 'em. Let's git."

The distant shooting drew nearer and nearer until it was very close. Then it swept on past and grew dimmer until it stopped all together.

Overhead there was nothing but silence.

He waited fifteen minutes, and then cautiously opened the cellar door and looked around. The roof of the house was gone and one wall of the house was blown out, but there wasn't a soul in sight. He pushed the door all the way back, climbed the steps, and stepped into the clean air and sunlight.

Longarm stood with Kyle Greenwood out in front of the ruined house. The barn was not only gone, there was a small hole in the ground in the general area where the dynamite had been. One of Greenwood's men had fetched up Longarm's horse from where he'd tied him out of reach of the dynamite blast. Lily Gail's buggy horse was cropping grass in the yard, acting as if nothing had happened. Longarm had no idea how the horse had gotten out of the house and survived the blast. Lily Gail was sitting behind them on the small porch of the house.

Kyle Greenwood said, "Longarm, it looks like you got seven of them. And that includes Vern."

"I don't know if I can take credit for Vern. That was the dynamite's work."

"Yeah, but it was you that set off the dynamite. Boy, did he look funny. Wasn't a mark on him except his clothes was blowed clean off him, including his boots. And him deader'n a doornail."

Longarm looked back toward the cellar. He heaved a sigh. "Kyle, I think this is one of the few times I've been hunted. I can't say I care for it at all."

Greenwood looked down. "I feel kind of guilty about sendin' you into an ambush."

"Hell, how could you have knowed?"

Greenwood shook his head and spit tobacco. "I couldn't. We may have got one more in that little chase we give 'em, but our horses was played out from that hard ride out from town."

Longarm nodded. "That's all right. I think I know where to look for them." He gazed grimly toward the northwest.

Greenwood reached out and touched his shoulder. "That shore looks like blood."

"It's tomatoes."

Greenwood was looking at him. "To tell the truth, you look bad enough to have been shot. Several times."

Longarm looked back at Lily Gail and said, "I feel like it."

Greenwood pointed. "What about her? What kind of charges you want to bring against her."

Longarm looked at the pathetic figure for a moment. Then he shrugged and said, "None. Let her go. It wouldn't do no good to put her in jail. She wouldn't understand why." He put out his hand to the sheriff. "Well, Kyle, I am much obliged for you answering my shout."

Greenwood laughed as they shook hands. "Shout? Hell, we thought the other half of the world had blowed up. That blast broke windows in Wichita Falls, if you can imagine. That wasn't no posse I had with me, that was a bunch of sightseers. Fortunately, they was all armed. It didn't take me long to recognize who was who and what was what. Well, you take it easy there, Longarm."

Longarm walked the few yards to his horse. Just as he put a foot in the stirrup he felt a tug on his arm. It was Lily Gail. She looked at him plaintively. "Reckon I could go along with you?"

He shook his head slowly. "Afraid not, Lily Gail."

She said, instinctively pushing out her bosoms, "We could git us a hotel room an', well, you know. Finish what we started."

Longarm smiled wanly. He stepped up into the saddle and looked down at the young woman. "Lily Gail, I feel like the tomcat humpin' the prettiest little girl skunk he's ever seen. I ain't had all I want, just all I can stand."

As he reined his horse around he gave Kyle Greenwood one last wave, and then started for the main road and Lawton and the train to Denver he was way late for. About a hundred yards away from the house he looked back. Lily Gail was still standing forlornly, looking after him, her arms crossed under her breasts. He felt sorry for her, but there was nothing he could do. He'd kept her out of jail. That was more than she deserved.

He turned toward the front and the future. As he rode he realized that he'd taken a chunk out of the Gallaghers' hide. But it wasn't enough. He might have crippled them a little, but there were two brothers left, and gunmen and bandits and murderers were easy to recruit. Still, he knew a great deal more about them now, and that would make the tracking easier. He had no intention of resting until he'd put the whole murdering gang out of business.

A thought suddenly crossed his mind, and he grimaced. There was still the matter of the report he'd have to turn into Billy Vail on this latest development and how that old goat would roar at the news of Longarm being trapped by a woman and ending up chained in a barn. He reached the main road and turned north toward Lawton, trying to think if there was any way he could make his report, give the facts, and somehow leave Lily Gail out of it. He honestly felt as if he'd rather be chained back in the barn than to go through the hoorahing that Billy Vail would give him.

He sighed and said to the sorry mount between his legs, "Horse, you don't know how lucky you are that you been gelded. I ain't in favor of it as a general thing among men, but I can think of a time or two when it might have come in handy in my case."

The horse didn't say anything, so Longarm kicked him up into a lope. Might as well get on back and get it over with.

Watch for

LONGARM AND THE APACHE PLUNDER

189th in the bold LONGARM series
from Jove

Coming in September!

If you enjoyed this book, subscribe now and get...

TWO FREE

A $7.00 VALUE—

If you would like to read more of the very best, most exciting, adventurous, action-packed Westerns being published today, you'll want to subscribe to True Value's Western Home Subscription Service.

Each month the editors of True Value will select the 6 very best Westerns from America's leading publishers for special readers like you. You'll be able to preview these new titles as soon as they are published, *FREE* for ten days with no obligation!

TWO FREE BOOKS

When you subscribe, we'll send you your first month's shipment of the newest and best 6 Westerns for you to preview. With your first shipment, two of these books will be yours as our introductory gift to you absolutely *FREE* (a $7.00 value), regardless of what you decide to do. If

you like them, as much as we think you will, keep all six books but pay for just 4 at the low subscriber rate of just $2.75 each. If you decide to return them, keep 2 of the titles as our gift. No obligation.

Special Subscriber Savings

When you become a True Value subscriber you'll save money several ways. First, all regular monthly selections will be billed at the low subscriber price of just $2.75 each. That's at least a savings of $4.50 each month below the publishers price. Second, there is never any shipping, handling or other hidden charges—*Free home delivery*. What's more there is no minimum number of books you must buy, you may return any selection for full credit and you can cancel your subscription at any time. A TRUE VALUE!

A special offer for people who enjoy reading the best Westerns published today.

WESTERNS!

NO OBLIGATION

Mail the coupon below

To start your subscription and receive 2 FREE WESTERNS, fill out the coupon below and mail it today. We'll send your first shipment which includes 2 FREE BOOKS as soon as we receive it.

Mail To: **True Value Home Subscription Services, Inc. P.O. Box 5235**
120 Brighton Road, Clifton, New Jersey 07015-5235

YES! I want to start reviewing the very best Westerns being published today. Send me my first shipment of 6 Westerns for me to preview FREE for 10 days. If I decide to keep them, I'll pay for just 4 of the books at the low subscriber price of $2.75 each; a total $11.00 (a $21.00 value). Then each month I'll receive the 6 newest and best Westerns to preview Free for 10 days. If I'm not satisfied I may return them within 10 days and owe nothing. Otherwise I'll be billed at the special low subscriber rate of $2.75 each; a total of $16.50 (at least a $21.00 value) and save $4.50 off the publishers price. There are never any shipping, handling or other hidden charges. I understand I am under no obligation to purchase any number of books and I can cancel my subscription at any time. no questions asked. In any case the 2 FREE books are mine to keep.

Name _____

Street Address _____ Apt. No. _____

City _____ State _____ Zip Code _____

Telephone _____

Signature _____
(if under 18 parent or guardian must sign)

Terms and prices subject to change. Orders subject
to acceptance by True Value Home Subscription
Services. Inc.

11435-9